Abc

Christopher Bryde was born in Alaska and served as a U.S. Marine Infantry Machine Gunner with 2nd Battalion 7th Marines Regiment in Afghanistan, 2008. He lost both of his legs below the knee due to wounds received in combat by a Taliban IED. He spent many years recovering and after retiring from the Marines, he began a life of academic study and charity work. After achieving two degrees at PCC in Portland, Oregon, he was accepted into St. Mary's University Twickenham London, where he completed his BA in Creative and Professional Writing and then an MA in Creative Writing: First Novel. As of 2024, he was enrolled at St. Mary's and studying towards his PhD in Creative Writing. He produced and starred in the 2020 documentary *The Forgotten Battalion*, which focused on the aftereffects of war and suicide epidemic which plagued his unit. He is also an Invictus Games athlete and will compete in the first ever Winter Invictus Games in 2025.

Upgunner

By Christopher Bryde

Copyright © Christopher Bryde 2024

Christopher Bryde asserts the moral right to be identified as the author of this work.

All rights reserved. No part of this publication may be reproduced, stored in a retrieval system, or transmitted, in any form or by any means, electronic, mechanical, photocopying, recording or otherwise, without prior written permission of the publisher.

This is the first edition of this work published in 2024 on Amazon's Kindle Direct Publishing.

ISBN: 9798336548556

Preface

This is a work of fiction. It was originally written as a work of non-fiction but through several years of work, it was entirely rewritten into fiction. I will say that everything mentioned in the book did happen and it is a true story, in so much as it is a true telling of what went on in Afghanistan in general. But the characters and what they did or did not do has become fictional, and in no meaningful way represent any particular individual or event.

Lastly, as someone who has struggled their whole life with reading and writing because of dyslexia and dysgraphia, I am proud to say that this is wholly a human work. No AI was used in the making of this book at any point – despite many people arguing with me and telling me I should use it. It was very difficult to write, edit, & format, and I am proud of it as it is and would rather risk error than ever lose sincerity.

Acknowledgements

Thank you to Dr. Karen Embry and Prof. Elizabeth Knight for encouraging me in my writing whilst I studied at PCC Rock Creek, Portland, Oregon. A special thank you to Dr. Richard Mills for inspiring me to develop my own life experiences into a work of non-fiction at St. Mary's University Twickenham London. A special thank you to Dr. Russell Schechter for guiding me in transforming it into a work of fiction. And thank you to everyone who helped along the way by reading and commenting on the material in progress. Especially the St. Mary's MA Creative Writing: First Novel workshop group & Dr. Conrad Williams, friends like James Wilson, Doc Mags, & Andrew Brodehl, my sister-in-law Heather, and my wife Laura.

For the dead and the forgotten…

1. The Therapist: The Abbey/Woman in the Window.

'We are going to start with an exercise, since this is your first proper session.'

'Okay,' I replied, scratching at my head.

'First, I want you to think about a place from your past where you felt safe and at peace.'

I scratch at my head.

'Once you have the place, I want you to close your eyes, and imagine that you are there, and explain to me where you are and what it is like.'

'And after that?'

'Then I want you to tell me about Afghanistan.'

I scratch at my head.

'I want you to tell me about one image that you remember that disturbed you or especially bothered you in some way.'

I scratch at my head and look down and to the left.

'After that, I want you to think about the good place again and tell me what you feel. Okay?'

'Okay.'

'Do you have a place in mind?'

I scratch at my head and look up and to the right.

'The Abbey.'

'Okay, now close your eyes, go to the Abbey, and tell me about it.'

'Okay.'

'It is atop Mt. St. Mary, overlooking the Fraser River Valley. The farmland below follows the river, and white mountains grow out from the valley in every direction – save for the South, towards the American border. The Abbey farm sits on the lower slope of the mountain and between the two is a Pond. There is a smaller pond near the farm – past the orchards, cattle, and the smelly pig pen. A single carp lives in it, but unlike the Bullhead catfish in the larger one, it will never take a hook & worm. Between the Seminary and the Monk's cells rises the bell tower of the grand cathedral. Inside the cathedral there are many sculptures made by Father Dunstan Massey and the colourful light from the glass burns and dances over them throughout the day.'

'When there is time for it, there are long hiking trails deep into the woods. Sometimes a Black bear will cross your path, but they are not dangerous and are only looking for berries. In the misty mornings, there are Blacktail deer grazing between the Seminary and the Pond, and often they return just before the darker side of twilight.'

'Sunday evenings, you can smell Father Basil's pipe tobacco smoke in the long corridor as you return from prayer to the dorm bay. On Friday afternoons, the smell of fish comes down the hall from the kitchen.'

'Each classroom can seat at least 50 seminarians. From the windows, you can see the Pond, the farm below, and to the right, the soccer and hockey fields. Where the window glass meets the wall, there are many names and dates written in pencil, pen, and Sharpie. When the tower bell rings, you can hear the taps of many feet headed to the cathedral for prayer, mass, or prayer.'

'I think we can stop there. It sounds like you feel like you are there. Do you feel at peace?'

I scratch at my head. 'I guess?'

'Now, I want you to tell me about an image from Afghanistan. A bad image. Something that still bothers you.'

I scratch at my head and look down. Some hairs fall out.

'You can take some time, if you need to.'

'No. I have one.'

'Okay, now close your eyes and tell me about it, like you did with the Abbey.'

'The valley of the Farah Rud – the Farah River – is a high desert space that stretches from the mountain footstools of the Hindu Kush, down to the Iranian border. Our FOB – Forward Operating Base – FOB Bala Boluk, was outside the town of Farah Rud, in the northeast. It is a small town of mud huts and a bazaar, all in the shadow of Safarak Mountain to the southwest. In every direction are brown mountains, like a cage, holding you down, into the space below. If you drive on the hardball – paved road – to the northwest towards Herat, just before you begin the ascent into the mountains, on the south side of the road, there was an Afghan National Police post. A concrete building left by the Soviets with windows and a wooden ladder to the roof. The corners of the roof are covered in sandbags and PKM Russian machine guns peek out at you from each corner. The post was manned by 13 Taliban masquerading as ANP – Afghan National Police.'

'We knew that they were Taliban straight away. You can tell when men have done evil things, plan to do more, and fear it being brought to the open. They have a darkness about them, they have trouble looking you in the eye, and there is no light in their eyes. Also, several of them had RPGs – rocket propelled grenade launchers – loaded with anti-tank rockets. NATO did not issue those to the ANP because they are designed to pierce armoured vehicles like our Humvees, rather than civilian vehicles used by the Taliban. Unfortunately, we could not kill these men outright – that would have been best – and had to play along like we did not know what they were. The best we could do was keep regular surveillance on them and hope we could gather some intel from their movements.'

'I'm sorry, but would it not be best to just arrest them, and turn them over to the local authority?'

'It was too corrupt. They would never have been found to be Taliban in Afghan court. Almost all of the Taliban we captured during my seven months there were released by the ANP. Sometimes after some torture and rape by the police, but most would walk.'

The Therapist scratches their head. 'Okay, so this bothers you? That you couldn't kill them, or realistically charge them? You were powerless—'

'No, there was something else that happened there. That place. An image.'

'Okay, please, continue.'

'One afternoon, we were doing a little patrol up the road to check in on the different ANP posts. We pulled up to that one – the Taliban one – but no one was there. The machine guns were gone from the roof, no men inside, but there was a woman. My Humvee pulled next to the building, and looking down from my gun turret, I saw through a window a woman in a blue burka, lying belly down on the floor, doing something with her hands. The Squad Leader and a few of the Senior Marines got out with the Terp – Afghan interrupter – and went in. The Terp was told to ask her in Dari what was wrong and if she would come with us, but she said nothing and kept doing something with her hands.

It seemed as if hours passed as they stood around her, hoping she would respond, not knowing what to do, how to help. By then I could see what she was doing. She would pick up bloody straw from the ground and then she would pull hair from her head. She was making a rope, and I could only assume it was – to hang herself. The vison through the window told that she had been violently raped by multiple Taliban.'

The Therapist scratches their head. 'That is terrible. Were you able to help her?'

'No, not exactly. We had been ordered never to touch an Afghan woman, even for medical aid. It was forbidden by their culture, and we were not allowed to risk offending the locals. In fact, this may have been why the Taliban did that to her – hoping we would find her, pick her up, and piss off the town and the ANP. And we could not risk telling the ANP to get her, in case they might do worse.'

The Therapist scratches their head.

'We were all silent as we left her there, driving back towards the Rud. But when we got closer to town, we saw an old man on a donkey cart. He had kind eyes and looked like a decent guy. The Squad Leader told the Terp to tell him about her and ask him to help her. He said that he would. We waited there on the road, looking through our ACOGs – rifle scopes – watching him approach the place. He went in and a little while later, came out half carrying her, putting her into the cart. After that, we left, and all we could do was hope and pray that he would do right by her.'

'So, this bothers you, that you were powerless to help her?'

'No.'

'Are you sure? In situations when we feel powerless we—'

'No,' I interrupt. 'It bothered me, and I remember it so well, because that was when I knew something was wrong – something was wrong with me.'

'When we experience traumatic things, it is normal to become numb.'

'No, that is not it. I already knew that I was becoming numb, and I was fine with it – really it was rather convenient being numb at the time. What bothered me was that the image in the window – of the woman – it had a strange beauty to me, like it was a work of art.'

'What do you mean?'

'It reminded me of Lord Byron's poem "She Walks in Beauty" – a poem talking about the beauty of a woman in genuine mourning for the loss of her loved one, and loss of her innocence. But more the beauty of the loss – the understanding of value – than the beauty of the person. I found it perverse and unnatural, though somehow attractive. Before this I thought all art was good, but after it, I do not know – it is hard to explain, but it is like I want to paint that image but know that I should not – no one should.'

2. Chaplain Thomas: The Protestant.

'Good afternoon, Lance Corporal.'

I stir in my hospital bed, attempting to sit at attention out of respect, when I see the shine of an officer's rank through the waking haze. 'Good afternoon, sir!'

'At ease there, Marine. I may be an Army Captain by rank, but by trade I'm a Chaplain. I'm Chaplain Thomas, and I'm just checking in on you to see how you're doing, and if your spiritual needs are being met.'

'Oh, well good afternoon, Father!' I said, relaxing with a smile.

'Oh, well, you can just call me Chaps. I'm a Methodist you see.'

'Ah, well that is two negatives you have going for you, sir. An Army officer and a Protestant,' I jest.

'Ha! Now that isn't very respectful for a Marine Lance Corporal.'

'My apologies, sir. They have me drugged up on Fentanyl right now. Also, I was always taught never to respect a Soldier.'

'Really? And who taught you that?'

'The Marines, sir.'

'Marines? Which ones?'

'All of them.'

'Really? Really? I've not heard of this before.'

'From Boot Camp, they teach us that we are superior to the Army, and it is a huge insult for a Marine to be called a Soldier.'

'Interesting, interesting.'

'When we get to the Infantry, they tell us never to associate with Soldiers, and not to salute their officers.'

'Well, I must say, I've never heard of this before, but then again, I've never worked with Marines before, let alone Infantry Marines.'

'You will get some respect for being a Chaplain, sir, but in general, we hate the Army.'

'You must not like being at an Army hospital then?'

'No, I hate it. First thing I did when I woke up from my coma was, I asked to be transferred to Balboa, and there I could be closer to my unit, but the Command said no.'

'That's a shame. Why would they deny that request? It sounds reasonable enough.'

'Burns. I have 3rd and 4th degree burns. All burn patients go to Brooke Army Medical Center.'

'Really? Another thing I didn't know. So how were you burned, if you don't mind me prying?'

I scratch at my head. 'IED.'

'I see. And was this in Iraq?'

I scratch at my head and look out the window. 'No – Afghanistan.'

'And were you the only one hurt in the explosion?'

'No,' I hide my tears in my hands.

'I'm sorry. Maybe it is best if we talk about it another time,' he puts his hand on top of my head. 'Do you mind if I say a prayer for you, even though I'm a Protestant?'

'Sure,' I reply, drying up some.

3. Father Jeremy: The Priest.

'Knock, knock, hello, hello, is there a Lance Corporal Brodie home?'

I wake up from a drug induced fog. 'Oh, yes, that is me, sir.'

'No sir, here, Lance Corporal. I'm Father Jeremy.'

'Oh, hello Father! Thank you for visiting me!'

'Which time? You don't remember me visiting you in the ICU?'

'No, I mean not really. But you seem a little familiar.'

'Yup, I've been there to see you near every day for the last month.'

'Oh, well –'

'Well, yes, the drugs they give you guys, I'm not surprised. Well, do you know how blessed you are to be alive?'

'I guess.'

'If you don't remember me, you won't remember that we had to give you the Last Rites four times. For a while there, they didn't think that you were going to pull through, but you proved them wrong!'

'Oh.'

'Yup, but all that is behind you now and soon you'll make a full recovery! Now I've brought the Holy Eucharist for you to receive, if you would like.'

'I would, Father, but I have not been to Confession since before we deployed.'

'Not to worry, Soldier, I'll give you a General Absolution, and we can sit down sometime when you are ready, and have a talk, okay?

'Okay, but I am not a Soldier, Father, I am a Marine.'

'Oh, I'm sorry there, Marine! My mistake! Won't happen again!'

4. Flashback: The Garbage Cat.

'You should have joined the Navy. The Navy gets the gravy, and the Army gets the beans, but the Marines, they get MREs, if they're lucky.'

This was the first thing my father said when I told him I had enlisted. The second was: 'Well, at least I know you'll do alright at Boot Camp. They couldn't do anything worse to you than I've done.'

I suppose he was right in both things he said, in a way.

Boot Camp, MCRD – Marine Corps Recruit Depot, San Diego, California – a month of concrete, yelling, sleep deprivation, yelling, concrete, hunger, yelling, waiting, running, concrete, yelling.

Then the bus to Camp Pendleton for a month of dirt, yelling, marching, sleep deprivation, dirt, tear gas, yelling, hunger, sleep deprivation, dirt, yelling, shooting, hunger, dirt, up/down the mountains, yelling, dirt, then back to MCRD for another month of the former stanza. Then, a Marine.

MCRD is next to the San Diego airport and there is an endless reminder of how you got there, and whether you made the right decision. All those people up there in the skies, coming and going. The only ones who look down from their windows and know what they are looking at are those who have stood where you stood, in the same boots, and who either graduated from it or yielded to the pain. Aside from the endless planes, there flew many seagulls – the only animal life of MCRD, save one.

At night, we would take turns standing guard of the barracks – practice for standing post in a war zone. One of my watches, I saw something pass quickly by the open door. Then a few minutes later, again – a cat! When I saw it again, I risked a 'meow' and it stopped, sat down for a second looking at me. I offered it my paw, but it would not come to me and ran off.

It was in rough shape and reminded me of a stray that used to hangout near my grandmother's trailer in Mt. Angel, Oregon, stealing food from her cats. She asked me to catch it and get rid of it, telling me she did not care how, and of how her father got rid of excess puppies back in the day – putting them into a sac and tossing them into the river. I did not do that. I loved cats, even nasty old ones, and instead had driven it out to a farm where I thought it could maybe catch mice and have shelter.

The next day, as we lined up outside the MCRD chow hall, waiting our turn to eat, I noticed the garbage moving in the dumpster next to us. Thereafter, I would see it every now and then, at night or in the trash. It would always make me smile and forget all the yelling for a second. I found myself relating to it in a way. Both of us were just trying to survive, and both of us were alone in our striving. It was all up to me to get through it, and to get somewhere else beyond just hanging on.

The last evening before graduation, I was assigned to stand watch over the platoon's green duffle bags, all lined up symmetrically/alphabetically, next to the parade deck. The same parade deck that on that tomorrow, we would all march our final march, becoming real Marines. Each bag belonged to a Marine, each potentially headed to a different job, and to a different unit, stationed all over the world. And each told the same statistic – 10% of your graduating platoon will die in combat.

I saw the cat again that night, but this time I did not offer it a meow, and it passed into the dark forever.

5. Hospital smoke pit: Motorcycle victim.

'Howdy, I noticed the Eagle, Globe, and Anchor on the back of your wheelchair. You a Marine?'

'Yes! You as well?'

'Err! And what you in for?'

'I am sorry, what?'

'How'd you get fucked up?'

'Afghanistan, IED.'

'Shit man, that's fucked, but hey, welcome home brother.'

'What about you? IED?'

'Nah, man. I deployed to Iraq twice, but I lost my leg in Hawaii.'

'Hawaii?'

'Yup, I was stationed at K-Bay on Kailua. Was driving my Harley back from the bar. There was some gravel on the road at a turn I'd taken a hundred times. I fucked up, lost control, lost my left leg below the knee.'

'Oh, I am sorry.'

'Yeah, it sucks brother, but these drugs they have me on are great!'

'They are pretty good.'

'They are even better if you drink some Captain Morgan with them and then have a cigarette. You smoke?'

'Yes.'

'What kind of cigs?'

'Newports.'

'Hell yeah, that's what I smoke! You got a spare one I can borrow? I'm Andrews by the way.'

'Sure, here. I am Lance Corporal Brodie.'

'Shit man, I'm a Lance too! But hey man, we don't have to be all formal with ranks and all that anymore. We're cripples now, we earned it!'

6. The Therapist: Ground Fighting.

'I'd like to start out again with a similar exercise as the first time I saw you. If you are okay with that.'

'No, I do not want to.'

'You did very well with the exercise with the Abbey, are you sure you don't want to give it a try again.'

'No,' I scratch at my head. 'At least not this time.'

'Okay, maybe another time, then.'

'Maybe.'

'How about this? We talk about your time in the Marines Corps, but before you left Kandahar, okay?'

'Okay.'

'Last time, you told me how bad it was at first and about your leadership, but surely there was a time when it got better, and they treated you better?'

'There was.'

'Are you okay with talking about that?'

'I guess.'

'Okay, then how about you start with when you first started getting better treatment, and why there was a change, okay?'

'Well, even after the normal hazing you get when you are a new Boot in the Infantry, I was bullied more than the other Boots.'

'Boot? Oh! That's right, Marines refer to new guys as Boots. In the Army, we call them Cherries.'

'Okay.'

'So, you felt that you were singled out for being weak?'

'No, it was because of my Catholic faith.'

'A lot of people in the Marine Corps are Catholic though.'

'Yes, but most of them do not take it seriously – not like I did – and so I was singled out.'

'Okay, go on, please.'

'It was not that I did not want to be one of the guys and all, but there were some things I refused to be a part of from the beginning. Others usually get worn down and give into the herd, but I refused.'

'Things like watching pornography – which they often did as a group – or going to strip clubs, and premarital sex with barracks rats, I always said no.'

'Sex with rats?'

'Barracks rats are what they call the random women that come on base and hang around the barracks wanting sex with Marines. It is very common. They even go around, knocking on random doors sometimes.'

'I see. Well, I suppose I can imagine why a young Marine might be thought of as odd for not liking that.'

'I guess.'

'Well, let's get back to the main topic then. When they started to treat you better. I am guessing it wasn't because you compromised your moral values?'

'No. It was because of the only thing all Marines respect – violence.'

'On the mainside of Kandahar Airfield, there was a USO building with computers and dial-up for us to use. The internet was so bad that it took about five minutes to open a Facebook page, but it was the only internet in Afghanistan. My Team Leader, Corporal Murphy, had taken me there and while he got online, I did as well but in a different room. After my 30-minute time slot was up, I went back to look for him, but he was gone. I found my own way back to the Marine camp on the far side of the base, only to find that I was in trouble. He was there with the Gunnery Sergeant and they both started yelling at me. Corporal Murphy claimed I had left before him and without permission. The Gunnery Sergeant said that I nearly got my Team Leader busted back down to Lance Corporal because of lost accountability. I tried to explain that I was there until my time ran out and that he must have forgotten me. This really ticked him off, and the Gunnery Sergeant dismissed us both and told him to sort his Boot out.

'Alright, but remember, we're supposed to be talking about when you got treated better, not worse.'

'I am just getting to that.'

'Alright.'

'He told me that he was going to haze me to death, and I believed him. For the next few hours, he made me run in full gear in the hot Afghan sun until I was totally dehydrated. Then one of the other Seniors came and told him to bring me indoors and let the other Boots do some of the work. This was when things changed. They brought me into a large tent where they had a group of Boots fighting each other. I was trained at Boot Camp in MCMAP – the Marine Corps' martial arts form – but I had never been in a real fight.'

'The style of fighting they did for fun, or punishment was called Ground Fighting. A form of grappling where you start back-to-back and once the fight starts, then you have to stay on your knees – no standing up. Closed fist punches, eye poking, or ripping anything off was not allowed. You win by submission – when the other guy taps out, or if you cause him to pass out. The idea was that your body was the property of the Marine Corps, so you were allowed to hurt it, but not damage it – at least not seriously.'

'First, they put me up against a Boot named Bo, who I had recently befriended. I told him I did not want to fight him, but he encouraged me to fight my hardest, or that I would just piss off Corporal Murphy more.'

'The fight started, and Bo quickly went for my left arm, pulling it up and behind my back. The Seniors were disappointed that he got me into a hold so quickly and everyone thought I was screwed. No one knew that I was double jointed in that arm and what he was doing felt more like a stretch than pain. We both struggled and everyone was surprised I was not tapping. Finally, we were both warmed up and sweating heavily, and I was able to slip free. As soon as I did, I got behind him, got my right arm around his throat, and got him in a blood choke. He started turning purple and eventually, he tapped. The whole thing felt like it went on for an hour, but they told me that it was under a minute.'

'Wow, that seems very barbaric.'

'I thought so too, at first.'

'So, after this fight, they treated you better?'

'No, there was more.'

'Corporal Murphy thought it must have been a fluke or that Bo took it easy on me, since we were friends, so he had me fight another Boot named Huntly. This one did not last as long as the first. I had a little confidence then, and I attacked him first. I got on top of him, pushed up his nose with one hand, and then got the other arm under his throat, and pushed his head down into it – cutting off his airway. They timed it this time, and Huntly tapped in 22 seconds.'

'Wow, so you were some sort of natural? Did you enjoy it?'

'I did, and so did the Seniors.'

'Next, they gave me some water and put me up against a burly SAW gunner Boot named Chad. He was much stronger than the previous Boots and I was beginning to fatigue. He got at my throat and started choking me, but I would not tap. I had made the firm choice to be suffocated rather than be seen as weak and so I struggled for little bit of air. Things started to go dark, but my body sweat, mingled with the sweat of the last two Boots and now his own, started giving me enough slime to slither free enough for a full breath. Once I had it, he was done for. He tapped shortly after I got a hold of his throat. He later said, part of the reason he tapped was because I was so red in the face that I scared him.'

'I think I'd be very scared myself. So surely that was enough. After that, they must have respected you.'

'Maybe, but they still wanted more. Even the smart Marines in the corner of the tent, put down their books, and wanted to see me fight.'

'They decided to put me up against Hector – the largest and fittest of the machine gunner Boots. He was near a foot taller than me, solid muscle, and prominent six pack. I was not in bad shape, but I was not perfect like him. What I did have – now – I was flowing with confidence, adrenaline, and activated testosterone. Plus, he had just seen me savage three of his friends.'

'This was the longest of the fights and went on for several minutes. Like Bo, Hector made the mistake of trying to get me to tap with armbars and contortions, rather than suffocating me. And even when he tried, my neck had become slick as an eel, and he could not get a good hold on me. I was honestly too tired to beat him, but I did not let it show and when I finally got on top of him and put my hands around his throat, he tapped before I could apply pressure. I was very surprised by this, but I took it and with it much praise from the Seniors. Corporal Murphy did not say anything, but he did not seem to be angry with me anymore. I shook Hector's hand and after that we became friends, and I became friends with the other Boots I fought as well.'

'Wow, it all sounds very impressive. Again, I think it is barbaric and not the right way to treat people—'

'Why not? It is fair. After that, I was never hazed again. Sometimes I would still be disrespected for my religious beliefs, but never again would I be treated like trash. I think it was fair. They thought I was a pussy, and I proved that I was not. What is wrong with that?'

7. Chaplain Thomas: Life.

'Good afternoon, Lance Corporal Brodie!'

'Good morning, you mean, sir.'

'Ah, you are correct there Marine. I suppose it is still five minutes to noon.'

'Seven minutes, sir.'

'Ah, well my watch must be off then.'

'Yes, it must be, sir.'

'So, they still have you all drugged up then?'

'No, sir – well, at least not with the heavy stuff anymore.'

'Ah, so you are just being a smart-ass, then.'

'Yes, sir!'

'Another thing they taught you in the Marine Corps?'

'No sir, I am self-taught, sir.'

'Ha! very well, then Marine. So how has your recovery been going?'

'It has been okay. The physical therapy has been painful, but they said that soon I will be allowed to wheel myself around and not have to be pushed all over the place.'

'That's great! I'm sure that you've been missing your independence.'

'Yes, sir. Also, they finally took the tube out of my – dick. And I can pee like a real boy again.'

'Ah, that is good.'

'Yup, it was not as painful when they pulled it out as it was for the butt tube. Less blood too!'

'Indeed – so, anyway, how has your spiritual rehabilitation been going?'

'I think that is a question I should be asking you, sir.'

'Come again? I don't follow?'

'I mean, you are the Protestant, sir.'

'Ha! Right, well, I suppose no one is perfect.'

'The Virgin Mary was, as was her Son, sir.'

'Ha! Very good, Lance Corporal. I suppose that Wesley would have agreed with you. So, have you been watching the daily mass they livestream in the hospital?'

'No, sir.'

'Oh, and why is that?'

It is not the same. Father Jeremy brings me the Eucharist after mass sometimes, but I do not watch it. It is not the same.'

'What's so different about it? You don't believe that God is confined to inside a church, do you?'

'No, no, not at all. Just personally, I am easily distracted, and I need a church for the kind of attention and reverence that I want to give to Him. A TV is not the same. I use a TV for entertainment and education. I want it to be separate from prayer.'

'I suppose I can see what you are saying. Though personally, I find that I pray better in nature than inside a church.'

'I get what you mean, but for me, it is like this, sir. You go to the rifle range to practice your rifle skill, to concentrate and improve it in a controlled environment. You go to the woods to shoot targets for fun.'

'Very interesting! So, you Marines make everything about shooting?'

'Well, I mean, it is easier to understand that way, is it not, sir?'

'I suppose. And in your metaphor, what would using your rifle in war be then?'

'Well sir, that is the easy one. War is life.'

8. Father Jeremy: EOF/Bloodlust.

'Knock, knock! How we doing today, Marine?'

'Good morning, Father! I am doing okay. How are you?'

'Good, good, all is good. I thought you might be feeling better today, and might like to have a Confession?'

'Oh, yes, I mean I am better, but I have not done a proper examination of conscience to prepare for one.'

'That's alright, we can just talk about anything in particular that is bothering you. That is, if you have anything that is bothering you?'

'Oh, yes, I suppose that would be alright.'

'Okay, In the Name of the Father, and of the Son, and of the Holy Spirit. Amen.'

'Forgive me, Father, for I have sinned. My last Confession was – well – before – before Afghanistan. Maybe in April – and it is December now?'

'Alright, and is there anything from those months that you'd like to talk about which is troubling you?'

'Yes, Father, a lot.'

'Okay, well let's just start with one for now. We can talk more about the others another day.'

'My first patrol at FOB Bala Boluk keeps coming back to me. We were four up-armoured Humvees. There were two M two 40 bravo machine guns – one mounted on Vic one and one on Vic four. The M2

50 cal – my gun at the time – on Vic two, and the Mark 19 grenade launcher on Vic three. We were supported by four Afghan National Police green Ford Rangers, each mounted with a PKM machine gun. Each of our gun trucks carried two to four Marines who could dismount and an Upgunner in the turret. The ANP trucks were overloaded with Afghan men in blue uniforms, each with an AK-47 or a machine gun. We would take them with us whenever we would go on long patrols. Our main mission in Afghanistan was to train them to be police.'

'We took the hardball east, over the Farah Rud, towards Delaram, then we exited North, into the rocky high desert. We were going to inspect an area where an Army National Guardsman had been killed prior to our arrival in the valley.'

'I was so excited to be manning the heavy gun and was at full attention – scanning the desert constantly, looking for snipers in the cliffs and hopping we would be attacked. I was so hungry for a fight I was practically drooling.'

'An hour passed without event, and we neared the area of interest. To my disappointment, there was no instant attack, no Taliban fortress. There was just a little mud hut village at the bottom of a hill. Some kids ran out towards us, and I got ready. But they were friendly, waving, and saluting us. A patrol dismounted and entered the village with the ANP, whilst the gun trucks staged overhead for support fire.'

'After half an hour, the patrol returned. The locals said that the Taliban had not been there for a month, and that they would send word to us if they returned. Our Squad Leader decided that we would return to the FOB by a different route, in case IEDs had been placed on our first route whilst we were at the village.'

'The route cut nearer the Rud, through wadis and over hills. We encountered several civilian vehicles traveling upstream. Each was inspected by us and the Afghan Police. Then there was a vehicle in the distance that, after seeing us, took off in the opposite direction. We gave chase, up and down, up and down, until we were spread out and my Vic could not see the others in front or behind us.'

'From the top of a hill, a civilian truck came speeding towards us. Corporal Williams, my Vehicle Commander, ordered me to stop it. I began EOF – escalation of force – first waving my orange flag. Nothing – the vehicle continued towards us. I fried a flare at them, but still they kept coming. Corporal Williams yelled at me to stop them. At this point, they were too close for me to do a warning shot. I aimed in my 50 cal, to show force. Corporal Williams yelled even louder. I could see the men in the car, and I felt internally that they were not bad guys – just ignorant of the rules. Giving them one last chance, I let them see me as I racked the 50's charging handle, sending the round in the chamber flying out of the feed-try and onto the ground. Then I aimed in at them – they, now close enough and with speed enough to damage us if they had a bomb. My thumbs began to apply to the butterfly trigger of the gun and right before I gave it full pressure – they stopped.'

'I could hear Corporal Williams on the radio, telling the Squad Leader in Vic one what had happened and complaining that I had not stopped the truck sooner. Then I heard him get yelled at for not monitoring the radio. The reason the truck had not stopped was that it had already been checked by Vic one on the other side of the hill and the Afghans were told to move on freely.'

'Corporal Williams opened the Humvee door, waved the truck to move on, and he picked up the round I had ejected and handed it up to me. He said nothing.'

'It was a 12.7 mm Incendiary round. On impact, it would have effectively exploded, killing them both. I would not have fired only one round. I would have emptied the whole belt into them until the thing stopped moving.'

'Well, I don't think that is a sin. In fact, it sounds like you did the right thing.'

'The thing is, Father, the reason it keeps coming back to me is not because I was proud of myself for judging it correctly and not killing innocent people. Had I wasted them, nothing would have happened to me. Corporal Williams would have got in trouble, and I would have got free kills – free respect from the other Marines for taking my first kill. I was both proud of not killing them, but also regretted not doing it. And I keep questioning myself – is the reason I did not shoot them because I actually cared about human life and morality, or did I not do it because I was not man enough to do it. Maybe I should have done it too. Frankly, I should never have allowed them to get as close as I did. And, technically, per regulation, what I did was wrong, and I should have lit them up.'

9. Flashback: Recon.

A lot of guys in the military think they are hot shit – think they are special because they have better training, more training, less red tape. Some of them are right, they are better, like MARSOC – Marine Forces Special Operations Command – but they are not dicks about it. In fact, all of the MARSOC guys we did missions with were really cool. But then there was Recon.

This small Recon unit pulled into the FOB one afternoon smug as dog shit. We had been out there in the shit for months and they pulled up like they owned the place, and looking at us like we were Soldiers, not Marines. We had lost a couple guys by then, killed loads of Taliban, and made great progress with the ANP and locals. These bastards came over, asking why we had not taken Shewan yet. Like we were incompetent.

Shewan was an area on the other side of Safarak Mountain. In the 1980s, the Mujahideen had dug a complex tunnel system under the area to fight the Soviets. The Russians were never able to flush them out. Now, it was occupied by the Taliban, and we had them same problem. The U.S. Army and Afghan military before us, as well as MARSOC then and currently, all had no luck taking the area. We had made some progress in the area around it, but Shewan was considered Taliban territory.

Recon thought that they were real special and decided to go in their first night at the FOB. The LT – Lieutenant – and Gunnery Sergeant tried to convince them that a night attack was a bad idea and that they should take us and the ANP with them as backup. They said no and went in alone with only six gun trucks. Within two hours, we heard them calling for help, as they retreated from Shewan.

They all made it out alive, but they left one of their Vics in the retreat. When we went back to look for it, all we found were some tire marks from where the Taliban had towed it away, deeper into Shewan. Inside the Vic was a load of high-tech computer systems with classified information, as well as a sniper rifle, explosives, and machine guns.

Recon decided to stay on the FOB and continue to support us. We did not like it, but the LT and Gunnery Sergeant were too weak willed to deny them. And despite their retreat and initial failure, they kept looking down on us. They would not eat with us, they got our Gunnery Sergeant to order us to clean up after them, and all they did all day was lift weights and eat. Always, walking around the FOB in their little black short shorts, with their chests extra stuck out, and noses stuck up.

10. Lance Corporal Andrews: Incoming.

'Yo ho! How's it going, Brodie?'

'Okay, thanks. Just tired from getting tortured at physical therapy all morning. How about you?'

'Not too great, man, they stopped my morphine dosage, so I'm going through withdraws.'

'Oh, I am sorry, that sounds terrible.'

'Yip, got the sweats, feel terrible all over, plus super depressed.'

'Newport?'

'Sure, man. Thanks.'

'So, what kinda music you listen to?'

'Well, I do not really, anymore.'

'What? You don't like music?'

'I used to, but I just do not enjoy it anymore.'

'Shit, man, that sucks. Well, what did ya use to listen to.'

'My favourite used to be Beethoven's sonatas – especially "Moonlight." It used to make me feel so much. Now, I do not feel anything when I listen to it, so I do not try anymore.'

'That's some depressing shit man. So, you used to like classical? I'm more of a country guy myself. Ya ever listen to country?'

'I will be honest – I have always hated country music.'

'Ah man, don't say that. What about Toby Keith?'

'I actually have a story about the time Toby Keith came to do a concert for us in Afghan.'

'Really? That's awesome! I wanna hear it!'

'We were at Kandahar Airfield, waiting to push West to our FOBs. The USO brought him out to do a show for us. There were about 1,000 Marines, several hundred Soldiers, and a few hundred military and civilians from different NATO countries. We all stood in a big open area on mainside and there was a small stage set up with an American flag projected on it.'

'He walked out wearing a desert cammie shirt and a baseball cap, carrying a guitar. They all cheered, and he made some very scripted speech about patriotism, freedom, America and that sort of thing. They loved it and then he got on with the show.'

'I do not remember any of the songs but one. They were all pretty much what you would expect. Something about a dog or a truck, the weather, and a girl. The one I remembered was called "The Taliban Song." It is a song about a good Afghan man and his wife. They do not like the Taliban and leave Afghanistan. But then the heroic President George W. Bush arrives and drops bombs everywhere, and the Taliban run away like scared rabbits. Right when he finished that line, four Taliban rockets came over the wire and splashed out close enough to us to sound like thunder. Then Mr. Keith ran away as fast as the Taliban did in his song. We all just stood around confused. I mean, you cannot run away from rockets and they only fire once and then retreat. Everyone knows that. We waited around for him to come back, but eventually we gave up and went back to the tents.'

'Damn man, that's a hell of a story! Though ya gotta admit, he is a civvy. What you expect? They aren't like us, man.'

'Yeah, I know. It was just how macho guys like him portray themselves, but then something real happens and all that talk means nothing.'

'Yip, I get ya. So, was that the first time you had taken incoming?'

'Negative. The first time also involved music. Do you like Green Day?'

'Hell yeah, man! I mean, they are hippies, but their music is great.'

'We had only been in country for two days. I was lying on my cot, combat boots off, listening to a CD of *American Idiot*, the song was "Holiday." A third way through the track and four rockets hit the old Russian minefield between us and the wire. They yelled for us to get down and put on our helmets.'

'Shit man, IDF is fucked like that. We got mortared in Iraq. They like to hit you when you're relaxed. It makes sense though. No wonder you don't enjoy music.'

'No, I do not think it was from that. Honestly, I thought it was fun when we took incoming. It made a fire in my chest and gave me hope that combat would follow, as well as the glories of war.'

11. The Therapist: The Team Leader.

'So, are you ready to try the exercise again?'

'Which one?'

'You know, the one with the Abbey?'

'No, thanks.'

'I think it might be helpful for you to reorganise your memories structurally.'

'Maybe, but not right now, please.'

'Alright, well last time, you spoke about how you were treated before the floor fighting.'

'Ground Fighting.'

'Yes, of course. Could you maybe expand a bit on that time before? Perhaps talk about your leader who punished you for his mistake.'

'Okay.'

'And maybe start from before the deployment. Maybe when you first arrived at your unit and first met him.'

'Okay,' I scratch at my head. 'When we first arrived at 29 Palms – first went through the front gate – there was a big reservoir out in the desert, below the barracks.'

'A lake in the desert. That sounds nice.'

'I thought so and was hoping it might have some fish in it. Then, when we got out at the COC, the wind blew up on us, and with it the smell of sewage followed. The NCO receiving us said:'

'Smell that, gents?' Whilst sniffing at the air. 'We call it Lake Bandini and if you haven't guessed, it is a sewage treatment tank. Welcome to 29 Palms and two seven.'

'Well, that is quite a welcome. So, this NCO was your Team Leader?'

'No. After they checked us into the COC, they took us down to the armoury and we were assigned our rifles. They issued me a M16 A-4 and bayonet. The rifle smelled like CLP lubricant and was heavier than the M16 A-2 I trained with in Boot Camp. The weapon had many nicks and deep scratches, the trigger had been replaced recently, the edges had been worn soft and shiny, and there was a hole in the buttstock from shrapnel. It had already seen a couple deployments to Iraq, and I knew it had killed people.'

'How could you possibly know that? Do they keep a record or something like that?'

'No, I just knew. I could feel it attached to the weapon. Like an evil pulse flowing from its history – like it had a special coldness to it.'

'And this frightened you?'

'No, but it should have, I think. Instead, I liked it. As I inspected and cleaned it, I meditated on it, wanting more. After cleaning, I was brought outside to meet my new Team Leader.'

'I stepped outside, where there stood two Marines, but I instantly knew which one was mine. He stood beneath the armoury steps, smoking a big cigar. Even with the steps, he was so tall that he still met me at eye level. His dark eyes looked into mine but at the same time, they looked past me, into the distance, and into the eyes of all the people he had killed in the past. He spoke deep and with a country accent:'

'Your name Brodie?'

'Yes – Corporal,' I said, after quickly squinting to see the ranks on his collar.

'You don't look like a gunner,' he spit cigar slime on the ground and took a big puff of smoke, then blew it in my face, causing my eyes to tear up. 'Whelp, guess you're gonna have to do. We need bodies. You ready to kill people, Boot?'

'Yes, Corporal!'

'Well, you're gonna kill em, or they're gonna kill one of our boys, you understand?'

'Yes, Corporal.'

'We're machine gunners, o three thirty-one, and we do most of the shooting. And it don't matter if you're dismounted with the two-forty, or are an Upgunner in the turret, we don't fuck up, or we get Marines killed. Understand?'

'Yes, Corporal.'

'You ready to die for the Marine Corps, Boot?'

'Yes, Corporal!'

'Fuck that, Boot! Die and fuck over your Marines. Don't fuck up, don't fucking die! And don't fuck me, Boot!'

'I won't, Corporal.'

'Wow, he sounds like he was a serious guy.'

'He was and he was right.'

12. Chaplain Thomas: The Therapist.

'Well, well, well, Lance Corporal Brodie. I see you are out and about and smoking now too!'

'Good afternoon, sir. Yes, they discharged me to Outpatient care. They have me staying in the Powless Guest House until I am independent enough to move to the barracks.'

'Very good! And how's your treatment going?'

'Physical therapy has been good, though painful. Mental health has been painful, but in a different way. They have me seeing this really annoying Army therapist.'

'Oh, Army then? I can see why you might not like that, considering your opinions on the Army.'

'With all due respect, sir, they are not opinions, sir. They are inferior to Marines, but that is not so much my problem with the Therapist.'

'Very well, what's the problem then?'

'The questions. Always trying to get me to talk about things I do not want to, but also the attitude.'

'Attitude?'

'Every therapist I have seen, they all have the same issues. They all think that they know what is wrong with you, and how to fix it, and that you are stupid and cannot figure it out on your own.'

'I see. That does sound annoying.'

'And this one keeps asking me to talk about the Abbey, but since I know what the Therapist wants me to get at and is trying to do, I am purposely side tracking, and not giving into the bullshit. I will only talk about what I want to talk about and not let them manipulate me into saying and thinking about what I do not want to.'

'Interesting, very interesting. But I would caution, and I assume, even Catholics say: Pride comes before the fall.'

'Yes, sir. I know what you mean, but I am telling you, this, this is different.'

'Hmm, well, you mentioned an Abbey? This is a place where you went to church?'

'It was where I was at Seminary, sir.'

'Seminary!? As in to become a priest?'

'Yes, I was discerning becoming a Benedictine Monk before I joined the Marines.'

'Wow, I've never heard of that! From monastic to Marine. But wait, you just spoke to me about it. Why not talk to your therapist about it?'

'I do not mind telling you, because you are interested. The Therapist is not. It is all about manipulating me into talking about things.'

'I see. But don't you think that you might benefit from it. Maybe it is for your own good?'

'Sure. Probably. And if they were upfront with me about the mechanism of it, maybe I would be cool with it. But I do not like being manipulated into anything, even if it is for my own good.'

'Well, alright then. So, how are you going to handle the situation?'

'Oh, I have a plan. I noticed in an early session that certain topics bother the Therapist, so instead of talking about things that bother me, I am going to talk about those – things that will bother them.'

'That doesn't sound the most charitable thing to do. Maybe, not the most Catholic thing either?'

'Maybe not. Maybe not. But after all, I am a practicing Catholic. Emphasis on the practicing part.'

13. Father Jeremy: Overrun/Dead Bodies.

'I have a few things to confess, Father – all from the same night.'

'Okay, and remember, you have the Seal of Confession. Nothing you say will ever leave this room.'

'It was late at night. I was sitting with some of the guys watching *Hot Fuzz* on a laptop, when an RPG flew over our tent and exploded on the wall. Then we heard the guard posts start lighting up the desert with machine gun fire. Tracers were flying over the wall and bouncing and ricocheting everywhere. My blood boiled with adrenaline and my hands shook with excitement. The Taliban were finally attacking us head on. I was so happy!'

'We rushed to put on our gear and everywhere you could hear the clicking of Marines checking their rifles. We got ready to climb the walls and fix bayonets, but then the Recon officer ran over to us. He said that we had to leave the FOB and go confirm a kill for one of his snipers. Bullets were still bouncing and RPGs hitting the walls, and this smug bastard was willing to risk our lives so his sniper could get a confirmed kill before the Taliban had time to remove the body. Just so his guy could get written up for a medal. Our Squad Leader told him to go fuck himself. Our Gunnery Sergeant had finally shown up at this point and the Recon officer told him to make us do it. Without a second thought, he ordered us to obey, and we lined up against the wall near the ECP – entry control point. Just then an RPG hit the ANP complex, and we heard them scream.'

'What I want to confess, Father, is hatred. I hated those Recon guys. They were all full of themselves and did not value us as fellow brother Marines. They would let us get wounded or die, for a stupid medal.'

'Well, I can understand why you would feel that way, but we must hate the sin, not the sinner. What they did was wrong, but hate the wrong, not the human.'

'I know, Father, but that is why I confess it. Because I hate them. I know that I should not, and I am trying not to, but inside, I honestly still do.'

'When we have strong feelings like this, sometimes all you can do is choose not to hate, regardless of how you feel. In time, it will dissipate.'

'I will try, Father. There is more too that I feel bad about. When the RPG hit the wall and I heard the screams, I started breathing heavy. My friend Hector even looked at me, asking what was wrong with me. It looked like I enjoyed it. I did. It made it all real for me. This was the real shit. This was war. This was what I wanted.'

'We started to open the ECP gate, and I was smiling. Then our Squad Leader was told to stop over the radio. A post on the other side of the FOB had picked up a mass of heat signatures on the thermals, just up the road. We were ordered instead to mount up in the trucks and surprise the Taliban. I was disappointed not to go out on foot, like we were about to, but still happy to man a turret in a potential ambush. We all got in the trucks and with only night vison and no headlights, we left the FOB, at full speed towards the little gas station up the road.'

'There were at least 100 Afghan males standing around it and when we pulled up, we turned on the lights and surprised them. To my disappointment, they all put up their hands and surrendered. The shooting in the desert stopped and no more rounds were fired that night on either side. Inside the gas station was a cache of AKs, machine guns, and RPGs, and several piles of ANP uniforms.'

'It was clear that they planned the desert attack as a diversion and had we exited the FOB – like Recon wanted us to do – they would have put on the uniforms, picked up the weapons, and came into the FOB, pretending to be reinforcements. Had we done what Recon wanted, they would have got in and killed us all.'

'Well, then, that sounds like you all did a good job, and also captured them without having to kill them. Is that why you wanted to confess this, because you wanted to kill them?'

'Not just that – I mean, it would have been better if we had. In the morning, the ANP released all of them. There were too many of them to process and since they were just in proximity to the weapons and uniforms, nothing could be proved. But that is not what bothered me most. After we zipped tied all of the prisoners, and brought them back to the FOB, I was getting ready for bed, and Chad came over, telling me there was something I had to check out. I followed him. Leaning against the wall near mainside were two dead ANP – the ones I had heard scream from the RPG strike. One had his guts hanging out, the other looked like he was still alive – eyes wide open like he was in intense pain. Some of the Marines were playing with the bodies and getting photos with them. I thought it was evil, what they were doing, and it made me feel sick. I ran back to the hooch and got in my cot for bed. What bothered me most about it though, was that part of me wanted to join them – play with the bodies, get a selfie with them. I am glad that I did not, but at the same time, I know why they did it. I had the same perverse inclination.'

14. Flashback: The West.

It was our last day in Kandahar, and everything had been packed into the trucks for our push West to Camp Bastion. From there, Golf Company would split up between three districts in Farah Province. One platoon of about 50 Marines to each district: Bakwa, Gulistan, and Bala Boluk. The other two seven companies would split between different districts, mostly in Helmand Province. Each FOB would be many hours drive from backup from another FOB, and since we were spread so thin, any reinforcement we might hope for would be no larger than a squad or two – 15 to 35 Marines. This was especially daunting given the reports that each district was imbedded with hundreds of Taliban fighters who knew the area, the people & language, and many of them had been fighting there for over a decade.

I was sitting out back of the Weapons Platoon tent, waiting for the other Marines to get back from chow, so we could take down the tent and pack into the seven-ton. I was smoking a Virginian tobacco in my Peterson pipe, listening to the same track over and over on a CD of Beethoven sonatas. The song used to make me feel so much and I had noticed that I did not feel as much as I remembered feeling. I kept listening to it, trying to find that same feeling again.

As I listened, again and again, I looked into the far distance – up at the grand mountains growing into the north. They were the footstools of the Hindu Kush. They were not like the mountains from my Alaskan childhood. Not white with snow or green with trees. They were many walls of used gold and old bronze, with brown jagged towers, worn and ancient. Looking at the hot wind tear at them, they seemed to sing in pain from the extremity of history they had witnessed. As if, since Alexander the Great to now, they had always known – it was only the beginning. They would continue to drink blood.

A tap on my shoulder from Doc Ramos took me from this thought.

'Hey Brodie, the Squad is back. It is time for us to finish take down.'

'Roger that, Doc.'

'Hey, what were you listening to?

'Oh, nothing. Just some old music, Doc.'

'Hmm, well you hear, I'm riding with you in the push?'

'No, I had not, Doc. That sounds good.'

'Maybe you can let me have a listen while you're on the gun, huh?'

'Sure, I guess, if you like, Doc.'

That afternoon, we pushed out West. It was the first time I had been in the turret, behind the machine gun, outside of training. I was very excited.

Only a few hours into the West, the two Kiowa fire support helicopters escorting us started taking small arms fire from some Taliban in the hills. My blood boiled seeing the helos light up a hillside with traces and rockets. I looked for a target, but I did not find one. The Kiowas slaughtered them like rabbits.

This push West would be the only time we would have attack helicopters for backup. Where we were going, there would be little to no air support, and when we would have it, it would be unreliable.

15. Lance Corporal Andrews: Boot Life.

'What's your worst hazing story?'

'Depends. Do you mean that I have seen done to another Boot, or that was done to me personally?'

'Why not both?'

'Hmm, well I used to be singled out a lot for my faith.'

'Come on bro, not just that. You're a bit of a weirdo. I mean, you smoke a pipe and read poetry and shit.'

'I suppose.'

'I mean, not gonna lie, bro. I would have hazed you.'

'I appreciate your honesty.'

'Shit man, any damn time. So, back to the hazing story.'

'Well, I suppose our first day at two seven was pretty messed up.'

'Fresh meat!'

'After we were all checked in, we were released to the Seniors of Weapons Platoon. It was a Friday evening, and they were all drunk. They called everyone out and then it started. Pretty standard stuff. We were each forced to the ground and made to do push-ups until we collapsed whilst they kicked dirt in our eyes, kicked us in the ribs, spat chewing tobacco on us, and poured beer over us. After we were very bruised and muddy, and a little bloody, they forced us into a barracks room, and made each of us bend over whilst they spanked us with a giant paddle.'

'Man, that's some gay shit.'

'Chad, one of the other, Boots laughed when they did it to him, and when they heard him, they pulled him around and punched him in the gut. After that they forced us to chug beers, rum, and other drinks – my memory gets hazy there. I woke up in the middle of the night after having a trash can full of water poured over me, but I pretended to still be asleep and then they left me alone.'

'Shit bro, that sucks. My first night at my unit, I got the push-up treatment and made to drink too much, but nothing that bad. Did shit get better after that?'

'Not really, at least for me. I refused to watch porn with the group and go with them to strip clubs and stuff like that, so I continued to be hazed for a long time. Really, until I was made to Ground Fight a bunch of boots, I was treated pretty bad.'

'Shit, that sucks, man. But alright, what else you got? You must have seen stuff happen to other guys too?'

'Yeah, plenty, but most of it is pretty standard hazing.'

'Come on, man, there's gotta be something nasty?'

'I did witness one thing that was really nasty, but I do not think it is technically hazing.'

'Well, shoot it, bro!'

'We were doing the machine gun range all day in preparation for our deployment to Afghanistan. A Senior named Corporal Williams was sitting next to me in the seven-ton Armadillo on the way back to mainside. He had just finished drinking one of those extra-large bottles of Gatorade when he pulled out his cock right there and started pissing into it.'

'Williams! You need to drink more water, Marine! That looks like diesel!' said Corporal Murphy.

'The smell of it made me gag and I turned away. When I did, I noticed Chad, wide eyed, watching the Corporal piss. The Corporal noticed also.'

'See something you like, Boot?'

'No Corporal!' replied Chad.

'What? You don't like my cock? You hurt my feelings, Boot.'

'That's not very nice, Boot,' said another Senior.

'Yeah, you really should apologise,' said another Senior.

'I'm sorry, Corporal.'

'So, you do like it!' said Corporal Williams.

'Yes, Corporal.'

'Well good, Boot. I feel a lot better knowing that you like my cobra. But say, how'd you like to drink its venom?'

'I'm not gay, Corporal.'

'Not cum, you faggot! I meant my piss!' said Corporal Williams as he finished filling the bottle to the top.'

'How much will you pay me to do it?' said Chad.

'At this, I looked over at him with horror, and the Seniors all perked up with excitement.'

'Well, well, well, we've got a little entrepreneur on our hands, gents.'

'You don't have to do that!' protested Doc Ramos.

'But, but I need the money, Doc,' said Chad.

'Now listen here, Willams. Ya gonna have the Boot drink that shit, you're gonna have to pay him a fair price, or ya could get done for hazing if the Gunnery Sergeant finds out,' said Corporal Murphy.

'Now, Murp, you I'm a fair man,' said Corporal Williams taking out a bulging wallet and pulling out a bunch of cash – mostly singles. 'Now Boot, this was supposed to be my stripper money, but shit, I can see titties on DVD. There's over $100 here in ones. How's about it?'

'Yes, thank you, Corporal!' said a seemingly excited Chad.

'Here ya go Boot, get it down. Every last drop too,' said Corporal Williams handing the bottle over me to Chad, who took it happily.

'All watched as he opened it, smelled it, and then began to drink. He seemed to struggle a bit at first with the taste, but he did not gag near as much as I was gagging. He got the whole bottle down and dripped the last few drops down onto his tongue. He then he made a satisfying ahh sound and burped, handing the empty bottle back to the Corporal.'

'Damn! That's fucked, Boot,' was the general consensus among the Seniors, and Corporal Williams handed Chad his $100.

'Man! That is so fucked! But hey, I get why you say it ain't necessarily hazing. The Boot got his reward. I mean, fuck it. If I needed the money, I might have done the same!'

'Are you serious? You would sell your dignity for money – and such a small amount?'

'Hey man, dignity is dignity. $100 is $100.'

16. The Therapist: Rambo I.

'I'd like us to try that exercise again today.'

I scratch at my head. 'Why is that?'

'I think that it will help you remember things that bother you that you are repressing. Repressed memories, I mean.'

'I do not have any repressed memories.'

'I have seen many Soldiers as a therapist and they always—'

'Excuse me, but I am not a Soldier!'

'Ah, yes, but that doesn't matter. Human beings repress things that are too traumatic to process, and dissociation—'

'I have an unrepressed traumatic memory I could tell you about.'

'Well, I think—'

'We were standing post at the FOB main ECP, and by we, I mean my friend Hector and me. The post overlooked the Afghan Police compound. It was your pretty typical duty that day. As the sun began to come up, a couple of ANP trucks rolled into the compound from the south. We watched as they pulled up, got out, and out of the back of one of the trucks, they pulled a tied up and blindfolded adolescent male – maybe 14 years old.'

The Therapist scratches their head.

'They threw the boy on the ground and one of them kicked him in the ribs, then dragged him by the neck into the station. A few minutes later, Rambo appeared. He was the largest of the ANP – at least six foot five and built like you probably imagine. We gave him the nickname Rambo both because of that, but also because he was fearless, ruthless, and an absolute killer. He walked over towards the ECP, smiled, and waved at us. Then he walked over to the gate and started opening it. This was a big no-no. Afghan Nationals were not allowed on our part of the FOB without approval. He knew this and did not care. He knew that we would not stop him. Hector and I both tried telling him to go and that he was not allowed in, and he just smiled back, pretending not to understand, and just replied: Friends! Friends!'

'He opened the gate, walked in, looked around on the ground like he knew what he was looking for and then he found it. It was a thick insulated wire about four feet long with one end cut and the other frayed to where the copper wire inside was exposed. He picked it up, smiled at us, and then proceeded to whip himself on the behind with it whilst laughing and exiting the ECP, back to his compound.'

'Hector and I both just looked at each other and shrugged. We were not sure what to do. If we reported that Rambo had just come through the ECP, we might get in trouble. Also, there was the copper wire – copper wire being an important component for an IED. But Rambo was definitely on our side.'

'So, this is troubling you? That you should've reported it?'

'Oh, not at all. We could not have stopped him without force, and it would have hurt the relationship between the ANP and the Marines. If we had reported it, nothing would have changed except that we might have got into trouble.'

'Tha—'

'But there was something we did report. A few minutes later, we heard coming from the ANP station a crack, like a whip, and then the scream of a boy.'

The Therapist scratches their head.

'Then again, and again, and again, and the screams got louder and with gargling moans in-between the lashes. Hector and I both agreed that we should radio the Corporal of the Guard. We did and he ran up to our post. He then ran down and woke up the Gunnery Sergeant who walked over and told us not to bother his sleep again for that kind of thing. He said it was their culture and whatever they did with their prisoners was their business. He went back to sleep.'

'The whipping continued until the screams suddenly stopped. Then there was yelling, and then there was moaning. Then silence. Just before Hector and I were relieved of our post by the next watch, we saw the ANP carrying something out of the station. It was a body wrapped in a white and bloody sheet. They threw the boy into the back of the same truck he had arrived in, and then drove off into the desert. Rambo walked out. He lit a cigarette, inhaled, looked up at our post, and zipped up his pants.'

17. Chaplain Thomas: The Cult.

'Lance Corporal Brodie, what brings you to this wing of the hospital?'

'Well, sir, the sign above the waiting room reads orthopaedics. So, perhaps the cripple in the wheelchair, sitting in the waiting room of an orthopaedic department, might be there to see orthopaedics. Sir.'

'Ha, well of course. And say, isn't today the Marine Corps Birthday?'

'Yes, it is, sir! How intelligent, for one of your kind!'

'You meaning by that, Protestant or Army?'

'Take your pick, sir. Take your pick. They are pretty similar.'

'Now hold on there, Lance Corporal. You can't possibly equate a Christian denomination and a military branch!'

'Oh, well, I suppose maybe you are right, for once, sir – at least with Army, I mean.'

'Okay, what are you getting at this time?'

'Well, sir, you see – the Marine Corps is not a military branch at all.'

'Oh really! And what would it be then?'

'Simply put, sir, it is a death cult.'

'Death cult?'

'Yes, sir. A sort of warrior paganism really. Whereas, and I agree with what you said before – the Army is just a branch of the military – like Methodists are a branch of the Protestant heresy. Sir.'

'Okay, well this is a new one. And can you tell me then, Lance Corporal, what could possibly justify the Marine Corps as a cult, let alone a death cult, and the Army just a – heresy?'

'Well, it is pretty simple, like I said. I mean, surely you know what our most common nickname is?'

'Jarheads!'

'Well, that is one of them, just, but the most common is Devil Dogs.'

'Ah, I've heard that too I suppose.'

'Do you know how we got that name, sir?'

'I can't say that I do, and frankly I've always thought it odd.'

'World War One, the Battle of Bella Wood, the Germans fired mustard gas on the advancing Infantry Marines. But unlike most troops that would flee or even die in a gas attack, the Marines kept coming at them – the gas causing their eyes to turn red and bulge, their mouths gaping open and dripping with foam.'

'And let me guess, they didn't flee because they were so badass?'

'No, that was not it so much as their blood lust. You see they wanted to kill. They wanted to kill so bad that they endured the pain and advanced into machine gun fire. The Germans were so terrified that they fled and they gave us the nickname Teufel Hunden – Devil Dogs.'

'Well, I'll admit, that is pretty extreme. But still, it doesn't make you a cult.'

'Have you ever heard us speak to each other, sir? Have you seen what we have written on our walls and tattooed into our skin?'

'Well...'

'Our holy sayings are things like: Have a plan to kill every person you meet. Pain is weakness leaving the body. The deadliest weapon in the world is a Marine and his rifle.'

'Yes, I suppose I've heard some of that, but I always took it as jest.'

'You took it wrong, sir. When you hear Marine address another, have you not heard the affirmation of: Kill! Rather than yes, or affirmative?'

'I have.'

'And if it is a very positive affirmation, we say: Kill bodies!'

'Yes, I've heard that one too.'

'You see, sir, Marines join for many reasons, but no one joins the Marine Corps Infantry that does not want to – kill people. This is most particular to the Post-Vietnam era, when the draft and forcing of men into war went away, and it became entirely voluntary. Most people did not want to go to Vietnam – all Infantry Marines wanted to go to Afghanistan – or any war really. When it was announced that there was going to be a surge of Marines into Afghanistan, this was not met with silence. The whole room of Marines cheered and roared with excitement.'

'Hmm.'

'You know, in our training, they make us watch videos of terrorists getting shot and blown up, children on fire, Taliban stoning women to death, Al-Qaeda cutting off people's heads with a dull knife whilst they screamed, and that kind of thing. It is all for a purpose. The more desensitized we became, the better weapons we would be. The less human, the more the machine/animal hybrid creature – that is what an Infantry Marine is. You see, it is the death cult of the Warrior Class, and Marine Corps Infantry is the highest order.'

'Alright, I'm willing to concede that there are some death cult like themes. But I'd challenge you on this at the same time. As a practicing Catholic, surely, you'd consider this kind of thing bad?'

'It is a glorious transformation in a way, but at the same, it does taste evil. Like they are slowly getting you possessed by a lesser demon, and once the evil thing is tricked to come inside, you catch it, not let it out, and use it – though it would always scratch at your insides.'

'I think I'll stick with my weak Army ways, thank you! And surely, you can't justify something that makes you feel evil, can you?'

'I do not know, sir. Sometimes someone has to kill some people – at least that is what the government tells us. Would you prefer troops killing your enemy who were good at it and enjoyed it, or the otherwise. We are the most superior fighting force in the world because of this – would you rather have the world's weakest?'

'Hmm. Well, I suppose that's why they say war is hell.'

'A hell of a good time, you mean, sir?'

'Well, maybe when you're in it and you're a Marine. Maybe. But what about this side of the war? You're still in it in a way, since it has permanently damaged your body.'

'Yes. Yes, that is true, but I still have the honour too. The honour makes it worth it. You know – you know sir. The reason I am at ortho today – I am discussing amputation with the doctors.'

'Oh, I am very sorry to hear that. I wouldn't have said that, had I known.'

'No, no, it is fine. This is a good thing. The limb salvage has failed, or at least it keeps failing, and I want it cut off. I was just saying – it is strange – in a way, I think I will feel more honourable if they cut it off than I do now. I want it gone because of the pain and uselessness, but also – I want the honour of it.'

18. Father Jeremy: Set to Burst I.

'Hi Father, I have a long Confession to make, if that is okay?'

'Oh, well, I have to get ready for a Baptism this afternoon, so maybe if it is a long one, we could break it up, and talk again in a few days? Is that alright with you?'

'Yes, Father. Thank you.'

'We were doing security for a MARSOC squad. They were doing a raid on a small village between Shewan and Farah City. I always liked working with MARSOC. They were professional, no bullshit, and everything you did with them was usually classified, which was pretty cool. Plus, there was always a good chance that if you were with them, you could see some action.'

'They had our gun trucks set up in a crescent moon position on the south side of the village, whilst they advanced in on foot. Our direction was to stop anyone from entering the village. We had intel that the Taliban had a leadership meeting going there, and that there was a high chance of enemy reinforcements once the meeting was broken up.'

'A while after MARSOC disappeared into the village, we saw several motorcycles speeding through the open desert, towards the village. They were about 600 to 800 yards away. The other Upgunners and I each fired flares at them, for Escalation of Force and when they did not stop, we pulled out our M16s. We fired warning shots in front of them, but they did not stop. With a car, when you are doing EOF, the next step in escalation if they do not stop, is disabling the car by shooting the tires and/or shooting the engine block, but with motorcycles, they are so small, you have to skip this step. We aimed at the bodies. They were so far away, I do not know if I hit anyone, and multiple Upgunners with some of the Riflemen, had all joined in the shooting. I saw the bike I was shooting at fall, but then get up and shoot off back into the desert. I could have hit him, maybe he was just mildly hurt, maybe he died later.'

'So, you have guilt about shooting at people when ordered? In war, you are permitted to follow orders, so long as they don't go against your conscience.'

'No, that is not it, Father. I feel bad, because it felt good. It felt good aiming at him, it felt good when I pulled the trigger, it felt the best when he fell down. It is hard to explain how good it feels, but it is like the best and worst feeling you can imagine, both at the same time, and it is so intoxicating, you want more. The realisation that you are shooting at an armed man who is trying to kill you, and it is okay. I feel bad, that I liked it, and I wanted more. I still do.'

19. Flashback: Nightlight/Numbness.

I was playing chess with Hector when the first red star cluster flare went up. It rose up from the north, near the Rud, and hung in the evening skies like some terrific fairy fly. Then came the yelling and all the radios on the FOB started talking. Two of our squads had taken contact with the enemy in the little village about five miles upstream from us. Our Squad Leader ran over and told everyone to load up in the Armadillo seven-ton truck, and that we were going to fuck up the Taliban. Corporal Murphy yelled at me to grab my shit and get loaded. I did.

The Armadillo was high enough that we could see over the FOB walls. Tracers were bouncing all over the valley to the north. Some from AKs, most from M16s and machine guns. Then an RPG would strike and flash in the distance. We waited, ready, loaded, sitting there longer and longer, wondering why we had not left yet. After 10 minutes, the Squad Leader jumped out and went to find the Gunnery Sergeant. He came back after a few minutes and angrily told us that the Gunnery Sergeant could not find his compass, and that we could not leave until he did. We were all disgusted by this. The firefight was within sight, and we knew the valley well by then. A compass was arbitrary – this was a bureaucratic technicality. Then the second red star cluster shot up and hung over the Rud – meaning a second Marine had been wounded or killed. We were dying out there, because of his incompetence.

We sat in the back of that truck for nearly 30-minutes before the Gunnery Sergeant finally showed up with the LT and his compass. As we drove across the desert, we ran into one of the Humvees from the other squads. Huntly was the Upgunner and he yelled over to us as they passed by that one of the Seniors had been shot in the head and they were evacing him from the firefight. He also said that another Marine had been shot, was pinned down by fire, but still alive.

We approached the scene at full speed, and it was like a *Star Wars* movie – tracers shooting and ricocheting, all over the village. But then they all slowed down and then suddenly stopped. The Taliban must have seen us approach and had backed off into the dark. We put on our NVGs – night vison googles – exited the truck on foot and formed a line into the village. We all turned on the infrared lasers on our rifles, which cut through the dark like long green lightsabers. Then I found a human body with mine. It was laying there, belly up – one of ours. Then my laser cut across a standing body with a rifle – I switched my rifle safety to fire, and like a perfectly choreographed ballet scene, I heard the safety clicks from every other Marine in the line in perfect unison. But we did not fire. We got positive ID – the body was a Marine from the other squads, and we all went back to safe.

We met up with the other two squads and they confirmed that they had been pinned down, but that the Taliban had retreated when they saw our approach. I wondered why the Marine on the ground was not being attended by the Corpsman and then they said that he had bled out 20-minutes ago and was dead now. We looked at the Gunnery Sergeant with rage – that was his fault.

We reformed and planned a counter offensive to find and destroy the Taliban. This was one of the few times that we had air on station, and the LT requested a bird come in and drop a bomb on the spot where we suspected they were fortified. We got a reply on the radio, but it was in Dutch. The NATO command was so incompetent, they had an operator who could hardly understand English. Eventually, the LT got across that we needed a drop. The issue was that the operator did not understand what we needed dropped on that location – they dropped pyro instead of a bomb – a giant flare that lit up the night like the dawn. Since we were all wearing our NVGS, this was amplified, and we were blinded. Now the Taliban had plenty of light to see us and how to escape. Our vision was all blurry like when someone turns on a flashlight in your eyes, and we were ineffective in stopping them. We looked for them for several hours after that without any success.

We returned to the FOB and found that the other wounded Marine had been medevaced to Farah but had died before he reached the hospital. As the sun came up, a bunch of us stood round, talking about the night. Both of the Seniors who had died were well liked – both by the other Seniors and the Boots. We wanted to cry, but were too numb – we felt nothing, but wanted to. The Gunnery Sergeant came to talk to our Squad Leader, and upon finding us chatting about it told us to suck it the fuck up and go do something productive. We were angry with him before – now we hated him.

20. Lance Corporal Andrews: The Opium Den.

'You know, they say smoking isn't healthy but know the guys who don't smoke don't make any friends and are all fucked up.'

'What do you mean by that?'

'Think about it, man. I mean, how many cripples we got at this shithole of a hospital?'

'I do not know. As far as Marines, I think there must be at least 20 of us. The Army must be in the hundreds.'

'Yip, and how many you know by name?'

'I suppose I see a lot of the same guys going to PT and in the hospital waiting for appointments, but I have not spoken to many of them – maybe five, not more than 12.'

'And where'd ya meet the five or 12?'

'Well, I guess right here.'

'The smoke pit! You make friends at the smoke pit. It makes perfect sense if ya think about it. It's fuckin' awkward getting to know people. At the smoke pit, you see the same face, at similar times, eventually one of you needs to borrow a lighter or a cig, and boom! Just like that, you made a friend.'

'I suppose that makes sense, but I still think it is probably not healthy.'

'Now, wait man, hear me all the way out. Those healthy guys who don't smoke, what ya think they are doing right now?'

'Probably watching TV or playing video games.'

'Exactly! They're wasting their lives, not making any friends, and not to be fucked up man, but if they outlive us, they will be lonely. What kind of life is that. And those are the ones who don't kill themselves, man. Man, a lot of these poor bastards are going to kill themselves.'

'I guess.'

'Man, I've seen it over in Europe where people still smoke. People are all friendly and have tons of friends, and why? They all smoke. Americans don't make friends anymore, man. They just argue about politics and act like cunts. It's fucking boring. People should smoke. It's more human. It's healthier even I bet.'

'Well, I do remember in Afghan, when I first started making friends, it was in the Opium Den.'

'Opium Den! Hell yeah, brother!'

'Oh, well, there was no actual opium. I just called it that for fun. Really, it was just a sort of cave made where two of the largest tents on our FOB came together.'

'Sounds like a pillow fort? I'm in!'

'In a way, but it was more like just a shaded area, with room for three or four to sit on sandbags. I used to sit there and smoke my pipe every day.'

'Pipe! Oh, man, I like the green stuff? Hell yeah!'

'No, no, I am not that type. It was a tobacco pipe. I never used to smoke cigarettes until the end of the deployment.'

'I bet they thought you were a weirdo.'

'I think they did at first, but then after I beat some of them in Ground Fighting, they respected me, and after seeing me in there fairly often, one of them came and sat next to me and we had a chat. Then more started showing up. Before you knew it, we had our own little friendship group. Almost like a club.'

'Kinda like you and me have here?'

'Yes, I suppose. Hector was the first to sit with me. He smoked cigars rather than cigarettes, so he was more accepting of the pipe. Then Chad and Huntly saw us chatting and sat down too. Then there was Bo, and we had our group from then on.'

'That's fucking wholesome, bro. Did any of your Seniors ever join you guys?'

'Doc Ramos would sit with us sometimes, but he did not smoke and would leave if it got too smoky. I suppose Corporal Diego did a few times as well, towards the end.'

21. The Therapist: Rambo II.

'Have you ever heard of EMDR?'

'EMDR? No, is this some Army thing?'

'No, not at all. Actually, it's a very effective treatment for processing trauma! It stands for Eye Movement Desensitization and Reprocessing. Basically, you see this light bar here. Well, you look at the light as it goes back and forth, and then start talking about a traumatic event.'

'That sounds really stupid.'

'Oh no, it isn't! It has been highly effective! I've read the studies and had this ordered recently! Would you like to give it a try?'

I scratch at my head. 'Okay, I will try it.'

'Alright, great! I'll get it started and then you talk about anything you'd like to.'

'Well, you remember that ANP guy, I told you about?'

The Therapist scratches their head. 'Yes, I do, but—'

'Well, there was this time we were with the ANP – doing a foot patrol in Farah Rud. Rambo had decided to come with. He did not wear a uniform like the rest the ANP – just a black T-shirt and a belt of PKM rounds – even though he did not carry that gun. He had an AK-47 which was spray painted black and he had duct taped a combat knife to it, like a bayonet. We were walking through the bazar, looking for intel. Normally, we would have the Terp tell the ANP to ask the local nationals if they had seen the Taliban or anything suspicious going on.

This was not very effective, as the locals always lied and contradicted each other. Rambo would have none of that. When he thought someone was lying, he would kick them in the balls, or buttstock them in the gut. Then one of the locals made the mistake of running when he saw us approach.'

'We yelled at him to stop, as we chased him down an alleyway. Rambo was faster than us and soon caught up to the man. The guy looked back in terror and ducked into an open courtyard, slamming and bolting the metal door shut. Rambo kicked at the door and when it would not give, he backed up, ran, and jumped halfway up it. He then crawled over and unbolted it. Several of the Marines and other ANP caught up and entered. I was carrying the two 40 machine gun and ammo belts and could not run as fast as the rest with all the weight. When I got to the door, Doc Ramos was just exiting it. He told me not to go in.'

'I heard from inside the sound of someone in pain – moaning and crying.'

The Therapist scratches their head.

'I asked him what was going on. He told me that I did not want to know and not to go in. I did not listen to him and opened the black gate.'

The Therapist scratches their head.

'Rambo had a unique style of interrogation. He – sometimes other ANP as well – would rape the suspect, Taliban or not. Then, after, whether he got information or not, he would cut off their dick with his knife and let them bleed out.'

The Therapist scratches their head.

'I had never seen a rape before. I had never even seen any kind of porn before and was a bit surprised by it. As the man bled out, I closed the gate, and went over to Doc Ramos, asking him what was going on. He told me he had seen it before and tried reporting it to the higher ups. Their response was that this was their culture and to forget what you saw.'

'And what do you feel now? Talking about it while watching the light go back and forth?'

'Honestly, I feel the same way I did when I saw it happen. I feel nothing really. How do you feel?'

22. Chaplain Thomas: The Turret.

'Hello, can I help you?' said the receptionist.

'Hi, I was hoping to see the priest for a Confession.'

'Oh, okay. I'll got get the Chaplain now.'

'Ah! Well, if it isn't Lance Corporal Brodie! I'm surprised to see you in the Chaplain office!'

'Oh, I was actually looking for Father Jeremy for a Confession.'

'You can't do a confession, chaps?' asked the receptionist.

'Ah, I'm afraid that's mostly a Catholic thing, actually. But say, Lance Corporal, if you aren't busy, maybe you'd like to have a chat in my office?'

'What about, sir?'

'Oh, you know, whatever you like. I mean, you did come all the way up to the 5th floor. I can imagine you might like a rest after coming such a long way, and with the heat today.'

'Yeah, okay.'

'So, how's it been?'

'Fine. Pretty standard I guess, sir.'

'Standard? Okay? What do you mean by that?'

'I suppose things are going as they normally do for most, sir.'

'Okay, okay, and how have you been doing emotionally? How's the therapy coming on?'

'Oh, that has been great, sir! I control the session now. Whenever I get asked something, I instead start telling them about something messed up that happened in Afghanistan. It clearly bothers them – the messed-up stuff. But also, they are not getting their way, and hearing about things that bother me.'

'Interesting, very interesting. So, you do have things that bother you though?'

'Yeah, sure. I mean, I was in a war. You are supposed to be bothered by things that happen, right?'

'I don't know about that? I mean who makes the rules anyways?'

'God makes all rules, sir.'

'Ah, of course, of course. I mean—well, anyways, so what does bother you though? Surely it wasn't all fun and games over there?'

'Honestly, you know what bothers me, sir? I miss it.'

'Miss the war, Afghanistan?'

'In a way, yes. But most of all, I miss my turret.'

'I can imagine having that amount of power and control at such a young age might be exhilarating.'

'Oh, it is. Standing there, the wild air of speed from the Humvee through the desert, standing there challenging your enemy face to face. You feel like the most powerful man in the world – able to destroy anything, anyone. And also, the restraint. You feel the power of not shooting as much as shooting. Restraining yourself from killing when you could, but it is unnecessary, or sometimes, wrong.'

'What kind of machine gun did you have in your turret? I know some of them are really impressive, though I've never shot one myself.'

'From Kandahar to Bala Boluk, I was on the M two 40. At Farah Rud, I was put on the 50 cal for several months. Then my Team Leader froze in a firefight – the Mark 19 jammed and he was unable to clear it. After that, they gave me his gun for the rest of the deployment. I was very happy about this. Partly because of the honour of taking his gun and having its power, but also, that Vic, Vic three was the one Doc Ramos rode in, and the VC was Corporal Diego.'

'They were friends of yours?'

'Yes, I mean, Doc was a Corpsman and a Senior, but we were friends and that was fine because he was Navy. Corporal Diego was the best Senior Marine. I would not call us friends, because that would be wrong – disrespectful – I was a Boot, he was a Senior.'

'You Marines definitely take that stuff more seriously than us Soldiers, but I suppose there is a reason for it. So, this Diego, what made him so different from the others?'

'He was fair and – he was kind. When I was being treated poorly because of my religious beliefs, he was one of the few who encouraged me. He respected me for sticking to my faith. Also, he was just a good guy. Normally, in my old Vic, when we got back to the FOB, since I was a Boot, I had to clean out the truck, refuel it, and then go on to my normal duty of cleaning the machine guns. A lot of the time I would not get to eat dinner because it all took me too long, and I would only get MREs. Corporal Diego would always help me with the truck when we got back that way I could eat. Doc Ramos would too if he had the time, but we were short on Corpsman, and he usually had to go straight to work at the clinic the minute we got on the FOB.'

'Well, that sounds like you had a great team in your truck.'

'We did, except for our driver.'

23. Father Jeremy: Set to Burst II.

'Hi Father.'

'Well, how about that! I see you're out and about on your own now. How are you getting along?'

'Not too bad, Father. When I was a child, I thought wheelchairs were fun, but they get pretty boring after you have to live in them for a while. But hey, at least I am not stuck in the hospital bed all day anymore.'

'Very good! It seems like every time I see you, you are doing better and better. And your Spiritual Life? I hope to see you at mass in the hospital chapel soon.'

'I will try, Father. But I am having trouble sleeping and the meds make it hard for me to wake up.'

'Oh, I understand, and you know God understands even more, but do try when you can. I think it will help with your recovery.'

'I will, Father. But today, I thought I might ask you for more Confession.'

'Yes, of course! Shall we pick up where we left off, then?'

'Okay.'

'A while after we had fired at the motorcycles in the distance – maybe an hour later – I heard a flare go up from one of the gun trucks positioned 25 yards to my left. There was a motorcycle approaching the village at a slow pace. On examination, I noticed that it had four people riding it. There was a man in front, a woman with a baby holding on to his back, and a small child holding on to her back. The other gun truck fired a warning shot, and then it entered my field of fire. I began EOF, waving my orange flag and shouting in Dari for them to stop. They did not. I fired a pin flare in front of them. Still, they continued. I then picked up my M16 and fired a warning shot at the ground 10 yards in front of them. They did not stop. Then Corporal Murphy yelled at me over my radio:'

'BRODIE, STOP THAT BIKE, NOW!'

'I did not know what to do. Maybe the man was Taliban, maybe the woman was, or maybe it was a man wearing a burka. Maybe the baby was a bomb, but – that was clearly a child holding on in the back. I did not know what to do, so I pressed my thumb against the safety, turning it from fire, to three round burst. I aimed in at the man. And adjusted for their speed. I fired. The bike fell. The LT, who had dismounted at this point and walked over to our truck, looked up at me in horror. Over the radio, I heard Huntly say:'

'Fuck, did Brodie just waste that family?'

'My heart missed several beats. But then I saw them get up. My aim had been correct, and my rounds had splashed out only two yards in front of them, causing the man to swerve in fear, and wreck the bike. He did not look at us. He just picked up the bike and walked towards the desert. The woman with the baby and the child followed him.'

'Well, that sounds very intense. But it sounds like you did the right thing and prevented something worse.'

'Maybe, Father. But that is not what I am confessing. The thing was, like with the first situation, when the bike fell, I felt good. And I think when they got back up – I think I was disappointed – disappointed that I had not taken my chance for free kills.'

24. Flashback: Corporal Diego.

By mid-deployment, we had started running out of bodies. Two seven had suffered over 150 casualties. 17 of these were KIA and out of the 130 something WIA, the majority were too wounded to fight anymore. And there were many others who were also injured but chose not to seek proper medical attention because they knew it would screw over the unit. Further, a significant number of Senior Marines had their contract end in the first half of the deployment – the Marine Corps would not offer them sufficient incentives to extend, and they left us. All this left many holes in important roles on every FOB, in every squad. And on top of that, our deployment was extended twice. What should have been six months became seven, and then eight. Everyone was exhausted, everyone was broken. We were technically combat inefficient and yet were required to engage in combat missions every day. This meant one squad of maybe 14 Marines, going hundreds of miles into Taliban held territory – no air support, often no medical evacuation available if needed, and if and when the enemy made contact, QRF back up might take hours and would not be more than another squad of 14 guys.

The Marines Corps, the Pentagon, NATO, America – they had all forgotten about us and left us to die. That is what everyone felt. But I did not care. I had the Mark 19 now and my VC was Corporal Diego. I had the most powerful gun in the squad and the best Senior was in my truck. Nothing bad could really happen anymore. Sure it was difficult and getting as much as four hours of sleep was rare. But it was alright. I did not mind the hardship. Having a position of honour and not being treated like shit anymore was so much better than before that I actually started enjoying the deployment. I would listen to the others complain and not mind. I could keep doing this forever.

'Brodie, what are you thinking about all intently up there? You haven't made a sound in that turret for the last hour?'

'Oh, nothing, Corporal.'

'C'mon, man. No one stares out into the desert like that who doesn't have something on their mind. That's just the way the desert is. It makes you think about stuff whether you like it or not. It's like a forced meditation.'

'Well, Corporal – I just, I was just thinking that I do not mind it so much being out here.'

'Are you serious? We've been sitting in this same spot, totally exposed in the middle of the desert, in the sun, for the last four hours, just because EOD can't hurry the fuck up and blow this IED we found.'

'Well, I mean – not so much this exact instance, just – Afghanistan. I do not know why, but I do not really want to leave. I have started to like it here, Corporal.'

'You serious, dude? C'mon, man? Don't you have family you are looking forward to seeing? Friends? A girl?'

'My family has not been great my whole life and I cannot say that I miss them, Corporal.'

'Okay, what about friends?'

'I have a few good friends who write me, but for some reason, I kind of do not want to see them again. I do not think that they would understand me anymore, Corporal.'

'Shit man, don't think that way. I've done this shit before in Iraq and came back. Yeah, some won't understand, that's true but some will be loyal and try. How's about a girl, Brodie? You got a girl waiting for you back home?'

'No, Corporal. Not anymore.'

'Shit. Well man, when we get back, you can come hangout with me in Nebraska. I've got plenty of family and friends, and I'm happy to share them. And I'm thinking of starting a business when I get back and EAS. I will need a good guy like you to come work for me. You interested?'

25. Lance Corporal Andrews: Tattoo.

'Got any tatts?'

'Excuse me?'

'Tatts, bro. Tattoos.'

'Oh, yes. Actually, I do have one.'

'And what is it? Don't tell me you got one of those Boot tattoos, like an EGA?'

'No, not exactly. I will show you.'

> **BRODIE**
>
> **K.T.   O POS**
>
> **574 XX XXXX**
>
> **USMC   M**
>
> **ROMAN CATHOLIC**

'I see! Your dog tag! That's a new one. Why'd ya get that done? You a motivator?'

'My Team Leader, Corporal Murphy, recommended it.'

'And why did ya get it on the ribs so far under your arm like that?'

'Because he told me that in an explosion that area is less likely to get burned or destroyed, and it would make my body easier to ID.'

'Makes sense, I guess.'

'It worked, too. That little $70 tattoo saved my life.'

'Really? How come?'

'When I got blown up, after, when they loaded me onto a helo, the MARSOC guys could not find my dog tags. The Corpsmen had cut off my boots and pants and forgot to take out a tag and attach it to me before we took off. The MARSOC guys looked for it and when they could not find it, they yelled into my ear:'

'WHAT'S YOUR BLOOD TYPE?'

'I tried to respond but the helo was so loud, and my lungs and throat were so burned from the exposition, I could not make enough sound. I then heard them say:'

'Man, this guy is bleeding out. If we don't get him some blood now, he is going to die.'

'But then I remembered the tattoo. I tapped one of them on the hand and lifting my left arm, I pointed to it. He looked and then said in my ear:'

'Fuck yes, Marine! You're gonna live!'

26. The Therapist: Rambo III.

'So, last time...' The Therapist scratches their head. 'Last time we tried the EMDR, and it didn't seem to have any effect. I'd like to again try the exercise we—'

'Oh, but I want to tell you more about Rambo!'

'Actual—'

'He was definitely an evil guy, but he was our evil guy. Well, that is what Hector said anyways. I never agreed with it – what he did. But some of the Marines thought it was fine and that the Taliban deserved it. I could not do anything about it regardless. But one time I almost did.'

The Therapist scratches their head.

'Sometimes the Taliban would hit the FOB with IDF – rocket attacks. They were not very effective and never killed any of us. I suppose they mostly did it to remind us that we were in the shit, and they were still out there. One time they did it when we were already getting ready to leave on a mounted patrol, and after it splashed out in the desert past the FOB, we sped out toward Mount Safarak to find the ones who set it off. Normally they set the rockets off on timers, but this time they had done it manually – or maybe it had gone off early by mistake. Either way, the ANP got to them first. Rambo got to them first.'

The Therapist scratches their head.

'There were four of them – young guys, not more than 20 years old. They ran. They should not have. Rambo jumped from the back of an

ANP truck, caught one, and threw him to the ground. The other three turned back to help him, but when they saw Rambo, they fled. An ANP truck cut them off and then another. They were quickly surrounded by ANP and AK-47s.'

'Their guilt was as obvious as their fear, and after they had been beaten by the ANP, zip tied, and wrapped in black blindfolds, they were strip searched by the ANP. One of them had the type of radio that was too sophisticated for a civilian. Another carried Swarovski binoculars – too expensive for a goatherd, which was what he claimed to be. Another had a bag full of Nokia cell phones – commonly used to detonate bombs. The last had tools and copper wires – stuff needed to make IEDs. This really pissed off Rambo. Recently, one of their ANP trucks had driven over an IED near Shewan, and it killed everyone inside.'

The Therapist scratches their head.

'Normally, Rambo liked a bit of rape, but he was so furious with these guys that he wanted to kill them outright. He walked over to my Vic and started yelling something up to me in Dari. The Terp came over with the Squad Leader and translated that Rambo wanted to have the Taliban guys run off into the desert, and then have me shower them with grenades from the Mark 19. We had recently also lost some guys in Bakwa to IEDs and the other Marines – including the Squad Leader – all seemed to like the idea. And to be honest, I thought it would be for the best too. At least they would die quick, rather than what would normally happen. But Doc Ramos said no. He said he would not condone outright murder and that it was wrong. They tried arguing with him, but he said absolutely not – it was not going to happen. They listened to the Corpsman and told the Terp to tell Rambo that no, we would not do it, and instead they would have to be taken back to the ANP station and processed there. Rambo was very angry with this and started yelling at the Terp and pointing at the Marines. When it was made clear to him that it was not going to happen, he racked his AK like he was going to do it himself, but then the Marines switched all their rifles from safe to fire. They did not need to point them at him, he got the picture, and backed down.'

'Later that evening, as we were getting in our racks for sleep, we could hear terrible screaming coming from over the wall, in the ANP station. It did not bother us. We all slept fine.'

The Therapist scratches their head.

27. Chaplain Thomas: Alaska.

'Well, hello sir.'

'Oh? Hello, Marine! How are you?'

'I am fine, thank you, sir. Walking by the smoke pit again I see? Almost like you were looking for me this time?'

'Ha! I see we can add paranoia to the list of your... hmm, well, how are you today, Lance Corporal?'

'As I said when you asked me before, I am fine. How are you, sir?'

'Oh, I'm right as rain, Marine!'

'Right as rain? What does that mean, sir?'

'Oh, sorry, it is a saying I picked up when I was a chaplain at Lakenheath in England several years ago. I suppose you don't hear that much around these parts?'

'England? That must have been nice? We stopped in Germany on the way over to Afghanistan, but I found it boring – especially the Germans.'

'Oh, it was! I love England the most of Europe. But say, you found the Germans to be boring? Why's that?'

'Oh, I do not know, sir. It must be their sordid history.'

'Ah, I suppose they did some bad things in the second world war—'

'Oh no, sir! I mean, yes, there was that, but I was referring to Luther and all of their heresy.'

'Ha! Of course, you were! I really need to be a bit quicker with you around.'

'Maybe, sir.'

'So, aside from your lovely time in Germany, was that your only time in Europe?'

'Yes, well, no. I went back to Germany at the end of the deployment too.'

'Ah, interesting. And was it just as boring that time or was it worse?'

'I would suspect it was just the same, but I would not know. I was in a coma.'

'Oh, I see. Well, we're glad to have you back on your home soil.'

'This is not my dirt, sir.'

'Oh? Well, I can tell from your accent that you aren't a Southerner, let alone Texan, but you're still an American. That's what I meant.'

'Not really, sir. I am an Alaskan.'

'Alaskan? I knew there was something different about you! But come on, Marine. Everyone knows Alaska was the 49th state, just before Hawaii. It's still part of the U.S.A.'

'Technically, yes, sir. But not really. Not from many Alaskans' perspective, and not from mine.'

'How do you mean?'

'We do not share a border with the mainland, but we do with Canada. We are closer to Russian than the lower 48, and we used to be part of Russia too.'

'Yes, but after the Alaska Purchase, it became part of America.'

'It did legally, but not culturally. You Southerners are all weak and cannot even fend for yourselves. Compared to us, most of you are like children.'

'Now hold on there, Marine. I'm from Michigan. I'm not a Southerner.'

'Michigan is south of us. That makes you Southern.'

'Alright, that is technically true. But we are not all weak.'

'I agree that there are some that are not, but most of them are in the military. In general, Americans are weak. They complain about minor things that do not matter, they do not know how to survive, they do not know what difficult means.'

'Alight, I will agree on the complaining issue and that most don't know how to change a tyre, but I think plenty of people have it hard down here.'

'Have you ever seen our winters? Darkness for most of the day, and in December, near a month of pitch black, when you might get a little sunlight for less than an hour a day? And that is when the blizzards are not set in, and when it has not dropped to below 20 degrees Fahrenheit. You will freeze to death if the firewood runs out.'

'Okay, I'll admit that sounds a bit rough.'

'Or when the wolves howl outside your door, starving in the cold, looking for a way inside.'

'Okay.'

'In the summer, it is all sunlight, but then the Grizzlies come out of hibernation. It was not uncommon or unexpected to hear of a neighbour being eaten by a bear.'

'Well, I suppose I can understand why you might think of us as like women compared to you.'

'Absolutely not! My little sister was catching pike in the lake and salmon in the river on her own at seven years old. It is not about men or women, black or white. Or any of that political bull. In Alaska, you survive, and you learn young, or you die.'

'Well, I think that is a very interesting perspective, but I must say, what puzzles me the most now... why did you join the Marine Corps then? Was it for the money?'

'After our father got injured and lost his job, we became very poor, but by High school, I had several jobs, and I was making good money. I had options.'

'Okay, well was it the G.I. Bill and the free college then?'

'No. Honestly, I have always thought that I was not smart enough for college. That was no incentive for me.'

'Well, from what it sounds like, it surely could not have been because of patriotism or love for this country?'

'No, it was not, sir. I think it was John Wayne.'

'He was very patriotic.'

'Not that. It was the idea of honour that he always portrayed. Not just his movies either, but also old Samurai movies – Kurosawa. That idea of honour. I wanted that. And I felt that it was honourable to serve in the military in the country you are attached to, when they are in a time of war. And that it was dishonourable not to and to let someone else fight or die in your place.'

'That sounds almost like a religious feeling of obligation.'

'That too – the Saints and the Martyrs. Even the living Priests and Nuns I have met. That self-sacrifice – that is not something I see in young men nowadays. Especially American young men. The only place I have really seen it, outside the church, has been in the military.'

'I see. And now that you are wounded, do you think you would do it all again, for that honour? Knowing all that you do now about what would happen to you, I mean?'

'I would. I would because of the honour that I have gained, but also, now that I have been there and now that I suffer as I do, I know that I can take it. I do not think that most people could, and I would rather take it on myself than have someone else have to bear it who could not. I can take it, I have, and will continue to.'

28. Father Jeremy: Set to Burst III.

'Hello, Marine! Nice to see you made it to mass today! Though I wondered why you didn't come up to Holy Communion? If I had seen you come in, I would have brought the Eucharist to you so you wouldn't have to wheel yourself up to the altar. I'm sure that might be embarrassing.'

'Thank you, Father, but I can take the embarrassment. I did not go to Communion because I feel like I have not completed my Confession.'

'I understand, but I have given you Absolution. You are permitted to receive.'

'I know, Father, but I still do not feel right. Not right enough for Him. Could we continue my Confession, please?'

'After the incident with the bike, Corporal Williams registered the mortar in the town for range. He was supposed to use a flare round, but what he fired was a High Explosive round. It splashed out in the centre of the village. Shortly after this, a bus came towards us from the village at full speed. I exercised EOF and they stopped without need of a flare or warning shot. A group of locals exited the bus and an elder approached us with a child in his arms – maybe seven years old. The child was unconscious and covered in blood. The Terp said that an explosion had gone off and they were requesting medical aid. Doc Ramos put a tourniquet on one of the boy's legs and bandaged the wounds quickly. He directed them to Farah, to the main military base, for further treatment, but we knew from the wounds and the loss of blood, the child would not make it. '

'After they left, the LT came over to ask what had happened to the child. Corporal Williams said that the child had stepped on an IED, and the LT accepted that. But we all knew that was not true. It was his mortar round that had done the damage. And I do not know if he fired it on purpose or not, and if he did, why he would do it. We all remained silent about it.'

'I feel like I should have reported it to Command. I did not because I did not want to piss anyone off or lose my new friends. I chose human respect over what was right, and I remained silent with the rest.'

29. Flashback: Care Packages.

Most Upgunners carry a bag in the back corner of their turret. Inside were gifts to give to local kids. Stuff like candies, crayons, pens/pencils, notebooks, and such. My favourite thing to bring was soccer balls. Whenever we were way out in desolate corners of the valley and passed a little village, I would quickly get one out, inflate it with my little pump, and toss it out. Then all the village children would run out and get the ball and cheer and jump up and down with excitement.

We acquired these items in Care Packages that were sent to us from family, charities, and random people who like to send stuff to military on the front lines. They were one of the few things we had to look forward to every week or two when a mail drop would get parachuted down to use. The packages would get brought in and sorted by whichever squad was on duty and then you would go check to see if you got anything.

Occasionally, there would be a mix-up, and packages meant for Marines in different platoons would arrive at the wrong FOB. This was normal and they would just get rerouted back. But once it happened that two packages arrived for two Marines who were in Bakwa. We all grew silent after the Squad Leader read out the names and then realized who they were. They had both been killed in action by an IED a week prior.

'Fuck the Taliban! Fuck Afghanistan!' said Hector, who had known them both from Boot Camp. He took the packages to the COC where they would be redirected and sent back to their parents.

I did Mojave Viper with them during pre-deployment, but aside from that training, I had not been with two seven long enough to know them on a personal level. It did not bother me that much that they were dead – not any more than if anyone I barely knew had died. What did bother me was the thought of the packages being returned to their families. The thought of someone's mother receiving a package they had put together with love for their son, and then – considering the Return to Sender processes might take months – months after being notified that their son had been killed, that package shows up on their doorstep, reminding them of it all.

Next week, two more packages showed up, and the week after that, two more, and the one after that, another two. Each rerouted, returned to sender. What would the parents do with the packages? Was it less painful the second, third, or fourth time one showed up? Was it worse every time?

The last two that ever came did not make it back. I caught Corporal Williams opening them on his rack, stealing the cigarettes, DVDs, and candy from inside, and tossing the rest into the burn pit. It was wrong for him to do that, but would it have been worse for them if they had been returned?

30. Lance Corporal Andrews: Camel Spiders.

'Evening, Andrews. You are up late?'

'Man, you got a Newport?'

'Sure, here. Are you alright?'

'Dude, fuck, I just nearly had a heart attack! There's a giant fucking spider in my room!'

'Oh no! I hate spiders too.'

'Man, I'm telling you, they never bothered me till Iraq.'

'Camel spiders, you mean?'

'Exactly! Those fuckers gave me arachnophobia, man. Fuck that! I'd take a rocket attack over finding one in my sleeping bag.'

'I know exactly what you mean. I had heard about them before deployment, but thought the Seniors were just trying to scare us. It was all true.'

'Man, I've seen one once... the bitch crawled out of a mouse hole while I was standing post. It was bigger than my hand, long greasy legs, with hairs. And those long dark fangs...'

'Please, stop! You are giving me PTSD.'

'I hear ya dude. Fuck 'em. If I'd been in charge of the Corps, as soon as I saw one over there, I'd say, you know what, fuck this place. Let's go invade someone else, with smaller spiders.'

'Agreed. Plus, I never thought we should have been in Iraq in the first place.'

'I wouldn't have agreed with you before deploying, dude. But yeah, I get it. It isn't like Afghan where we are trying to liberate them from the Taliban. With Iraq, we just said, you know what Saddam, we've had enough of your shit. Fuck you guy, here's some bombs. Oh, and while we're at it, an invasion.'

'Yup, pretty much.'

'Wait, so you had Camels spi... you had those big fuckers over there too? I've never heard that from other Afghan pump guys before?'

'I never saw them in Kandahar, but when we got to Farah Province, they were there.'

'What was your first interaction with them?'

'Hmm, there are a few main ones I can remember. Maybe the first was when we were watching the *Notebook*.'

'Hahahahaha, that fucking movie! Man, I remember thinking it was gay as shit before I deployed, but you spend some time in the sand, and ya have nothing else to watch, and boom, you're into that shit.'

'I honestly never finished it. There were about 15 of us, all crowded around Doc Ramos's laptop in the dark.'

'Shit man, so damn wholesome! I miss those days. Sitting with your Marines, all crowded around someone's laptop, watching something you'd normally never give a chance. Good times, man.'

'Yeah, I agree. We were in a war and terrible things were going on every day, but times like that it was like we were a family.'

'So, what happened? The thing crawls up on the screen or some shit?'

'No, my friend Hector was sitting next to me, and all of a sudden, he screams like a girl, gets up and runs out the hooch. We were all confused, and someone turned on the lights, and there it was. Like yours, it was bigger than a hand, like a facehugger from *Alien*. It had crawled up his leg and he noticed it when it got on his lap. When he ran, he must have stepped on some of its legs – it was running around in a circle because of it.'

'Fuck that, man! Fuck that!'

'Then Corporal Murphy got out his bottle of AXE body spray and a lighter. He lit it up and I could swear you could hear the thing scream as it burned. Then he went to step on it, but it ran away, under the tent wall and into the dark. Then we heard Hector scream again.'

'Fuck, man. Did it die?'

'It did. In the morning, I was walking to take a piss and saw the corpse. I kept my distance. For the next week, whenever I needed to piss, I would walk the long way around.'

31. The Therapist: Slaves.

'I'd like it if this time we talked about the night—'

'You know, the mayor of Farah had slaves. Not indentured servants or poorly paid maids, but actual slaves in chains and a metal collar around their necks.'

The Therapist scratches their head.

'We had to take the LT to Farah City one day so he could negotiate something with the mayor. I always liked to go to Farah, because of the castle. It is called the Citadel of Alexander the Great, from when he invaded Afghanistan back in 330 BC. Little remains of its glory, but the walls are still there. They are really very impressive.'

'Oh! That sounds very nice—'

'Always, we pulled into the mayor's home – more like a palace. Most Afghans in Farah Province live in mud huts like you have seen on Tatooine in *Star Wars*. Not the mayor. He had a nice walled estate, with palm trees, a garden, and a water feature in the centre. This was kept nice and tidy by the slaves, and all guarded by ANP. The mayor invited us all in for a meal. We wanted to go, but a few of us felt it was wrong, being survived by slaves, and stayed with the Vics, eating MREs.'

'Later, a couple ANP wearing man dresses came out and offered us some shit bread, which we happily accepted. Then they brought out a little boy who carried a tray of chai tea for us. It was nice tea. They asked us if we would like the boy to dance for us.'

The Therapist scratches their head.

'We thought that was strange and said no, which from their expressions, they thought the denial strange. They sent the boy away, and started smiling, and whispering to each other. Then they started giggling and making the in-and-out motion with their fingers at us, saying:'

'Fucky, fucky? Fucky, fucky?'

'We politely declined the invitation for butt sex with them, but they were very confident. One of them had a little bulge poking out from his dress and he went up behind Doc Ramos and poked him with it in the back. Doc Ramos got up and told him to fuck off, and the rest of us grabbed our rifles and did the same. They jumped back but kept smiling. They walked away, whilst giggling, and turning back, making kissing sounds.'

The Therapist scratches their head.

'A while later – still waiting for the LT to finish his meeting – we heard grunting, moaning, and crying sounds coming from the other side of the compound. Hector, Doc Ramos, and I decided to inspect it. When we walked over, following the sounds, we found a sandbag post near an entrance to the grounds. Inside were six ANP, four of them with their pants down, one of them was raping the little chai boy. The two from earlier were also in the queue. They smiled wide when they saw us.'

The Therapist scratches their head.

'The thing was, we could not do anything about it. Of course, you would want to stop it and help the child – kill the rapers. But we had been ordered that this was their culture. After we walked away from it, I spoke to Hector and Doc Ramos about it. At the end of the day, it seemed that this government we were over there to help was no better than the Taliban. Really, the only difference between them and the Taliban it seemed, was that they would allow women to be educated, and the Taliban would not. We decided that must be what the war was all about, or, rather, it was the only thing we could hold on to in order to justify the sacrifice of fighting over there.'

32. Chaplain Thomas: Of Troy.

'Ah! Well, if it isn't Lance Corporal Brodie! I'm surprised to see you in the Chaplain office!'

'Oh, I am not here for you, sir. I am looking for Father Jeremy.'

'Ah ha, well of course. Well, I'm afraid to inform you that Jeremy is at Lackland today for a conference.'

'Lackland?'

'The Air Force base. It's on the west side of San Antonio.'

'Air Force – disgusting.'

'Oh, so you hate Air Force too then?'

'Well, they are at least cleaner than Soldiers, but they are not real military – basically civilians who occasionally wear a uniform.'

'Ha! Well, I'll admit, even us Army trash don't think of them as quite military. We even call them the Chair Force.'

'Very good, sir! Maybe there is hope for you after all.'

'Indeed. So, since Jeremy is out—'

'Father Jeremy.'

'Yes, that's who I meant. So, since he is out today, is there anything I can help you with spiritually?'

'I doubt it, sir. I was going to ask him if he could recommend some good spiritual reading.'

'Ah! A Marine that can read! Fantastic!'

'Very funny, sir. You know we have a higher standard to join than you Soldiers.'

'Yes, yes. So, what do you like to read?'

'Well, I prefer anything classic. Personally, I think that if it is not at least 50 years old, it is not worth reading. Preferably over 100 years though.'

'Very interesting, and another thing we agree on. Most of this modern stuff is all emotion, not instruction. Is there anything particular you are reading currently?'

'Well, I took four books with me to Afghanistan, but they have not returned them to me yet. I do not have any here currently.'

'Hmm, would you mind telling me what you took with you?'

'Sure. I took *Orthodoxy* by G.K. Chesterton.'

'I've heard a lot about Chesterton, but never have gotten around to reading him.'

'Oh, you should sir. Like Newman, he was a very intelligent Protestant, who eventually converted back to the True Faith.'

'Indeed. So, you enjoyed *Orthodoxy* then?'

'Honestly, sir, I let a friend borrow whilst I was reading *Beowulf*, but he got killed, so I never got it back, and never read it.'

'Oh, well I'm sorry. Hmm, *Beowulf*. I read that one in high school. I recall really enjoying it.'

'Yeah, it is great. I have read it several times now and multiple translations.'

'Alright, that's a good one. What else?'

'The complete works of Emily Dickinson. She is my favourite poet.'

'Ah, I'll admit, I don't know if I ever read her. Though, aside from the Psalms, I've not read much poetry. Another deficiency to me, I suppose.'

'I suppose as well, sir.'

'And what else, what was the fourth book?'

'Oh, that was the *Iliad*.'

'Homer! You know, I have read the *Odyssey* but haven't gotten round to the *Iliad* yet. I imagine it isn't quite the same as that Brad Pitt movie based on it?'

'*Troy*.'

'Yes, that's the one. Great film, but I'm sure the *Iliad* must be superior?'

'Honestly, sir, I never finished it.'

'Really? You don't seem like a quitter. What was it, too long?'

'No. I really wanted to read it, and I see myself as deficient for not finishing it.'

'Was it the prose, then? Personally, I struggle with getting into some of the old Greek stuff.'

'No, sir. It was—it was not that. It was a name in it. It was repeated too many times, and I had to put it down. Every time I tried to read it, I had to put it down.'

'Name? I'm afraid I don't understand.'

'I used to date this girl. Before the Marines. Her name was the same name as the character in the book. It hurt me too much to read her name. I cannot read it, even now.'

33. Father Jeremy: Extended.

'When I was at the Seminary, we studied St. Augustine and St. Thomas Aquinas, and the idea of Just War Theory.'

'Oh! That's good stuff! Well, I mean, good that you learned about it, anyways. Most High school students don't learn anything about ethics nowadays.'

'Yes, Father, but I had a question for you regarding a difference between Augustine and Aquinas on authority.'

'Oh, yes! Very interesting! Go on, please.'

'I could be remembering this wrong, but from what I remember, Augustine says that if you are ordered to do something, and obey it, then any moral ramifications fall on the one in authority – the higher ranked one who ordered it, rather than the lower ranked individual following the order. Whereas, Aquinas says that you cannot follow an order, if it goes against your conscience, and you know it to be wrong.'

'Okay, I must admit, I can't say I am particularly up to date on my *Summa*, and I haven't read the *Confessions* since Seminary as well. That was in the 70s. But, I mean, it sounds pretty spot on.'

'Which one, Father? Augustine's view or Aquinas?'

'Ah, that's a difficult question, Marine. Can I ask why you are thinking about this?'

'Well, Father, it is about a time that I am not sure if I need to confess it or not. I am not sure if I did wrong or not, or if I am still doing wrong now, by not reporting it as a War Crime.'

'Alright, well, tell me if you like, and we can have a think on it.'

'We had been extended twice. We should have only been deployed to Afghanistan for six months, but then the Pentagon decided to extend us to seven, and finally to eight months. It was terrible for morale. We had lost so many guys – a lot of KIAs and over a hundred WIAs. Also, many of our best Seniors had their contracts end and they went home. We had not received any reinforcements; we had no air support and were low on supplies. We were considered combat inefficient too, but still had to engage in combat missions. The guys felt forgotten and started losing their standards and discipline. There was complacency and the gradual decline in adherence to the rules.'

'I heard from Hector and Bo that their squads had started doing some things that would definitely be considered intentional War Crimes. Our squad had been doing alright, but there was one day when things were not so good.'

'It was a standard mounted patrol out in the desert to the north of the FOB – the same direction we had recently taken fire from when the Taliban tried to overrun us. We stopped any vehicle crossing the plain and checked them for information. A small car approached us, but then upon seeing us started to turn around. We chased them down, encircled them, and four young men slowly got out, with their hands up. They kept their eyes down like guilty children, or someone who has just been talking behind your back and will not look you in the eyes when they run into you. The teams dismounted and the Terp yelled at them to lay down in the sand. The Marines then zip tied them and began to question them.'

'In a way, it was their fault. They have similar training to us when captured. You do not divulge important information. You are supposed to tell little things, stupid things, to make the enemy think they caught some of the stupid, lower ranked individuals. But you never remain silent. That just pisses off your captors – which it did. One of the

Seniors stood up the prisoner on the end, and then hit him in the guts with the buttstock of his M16. Then the others put the kid up against a Humvee and took turns punching him. A captive on the ground started yelling something to his companion and then took a boot to the face from one of the Marines. The other two started crying. Each of them were then blindfolded and pulled 20 yards apart from one another – so they could not communicate with each other and pushed down to their knees. The Marines went to each of them, one by one, yelling at them, kicking them in the balls, kicking them in the back, in the head. The Terp did the same, but then took his AK and buttstocked one in the face, knocking him out. He would have smashed his skull in with it, if he was not stopped by the Squad Leader.'

'They pulled the first one, the kid they had punched a lot, over and took off his blindfold, showing him the bleeding and unconscious one. The Terp told him they had killed him, and that he was next if he did not talk. Then the Terp wiped his hand over the bloody wound of the unconscious one and then smeared the blood on the kid's face. He started sobbing muddy, bloody tears. Then they dragged him over to my vehicle. They put his head under the tyre and told Corporal Williams to inch the Vic forward slowly. The kid screamed as the pressure came on, the tyre pushing his head slowly into the sand. Corporal Diego told them to stop and that he did not want towelhead brains splattered all over his truck. Corporal Williams reversed and the screams turned back into sobs. Then the Squad Leader and other Marines dragged him in front of the truck and pushed him down onto his knees, pointing up to my turret. They told me to take the Mark 19 to condition one and aim it in on the kid. I racked the charging handles. Then they backed away from him. They told the Terp to tell him that if he did not talk right then, I would shoot him. I thought they were bluffing, but then the Squad Leader yelled up to me, telling me that he would count down from 10 and to zero, and at zero I was to fire a single round into him.'

'A 40mm round is designed to only explode after it spins so many times – that way if it is fired at close range, it will not kill or injure the gunner. This was close range – five yards. The round would hit him and rather than explode, it wound punch a hole through him. I could not aim for the head, in case it was off a bit, so centre mass was best. I aimed where the chest meets the stomach, and the Squad Leader counted down from ten – the Terp also counting down with him in Dari. When we got to two, my heart skipped a beat, and I put my thumbs on the butterfly trigger – but he stopped counting. The LT had come over the radio, asking for a SitRep. The Squad Leader reported that they had captured four Taliban, and the LT order us to take them back to the FOB immediately. We did.'

'Well, that sounds like God intervened there in everyone's favour.'

'The issue I have here, Father, is that on other occasions, I usually resisted the blood lust. In that situation, I was not going to. I was going to follow my orders, and I liked it. I knew that it was wrong. I knew what they were doing was wrong and what I was about to do was wrong, but I was going to do it anyways.'

'Well, these are very hard questions for a young man. War is hell and there are no easy answers for these questions, I think.'

'That is why I asked about Augustine and Aquinas. One says it is my leader's fault, the other says it is mine too. And still, should I have reported it? Had I, the LT might not have taken my side, and they could have turned on me. Even if he did, I still would not have been safe. I would have never been trusted again and would have been alone again. Maybe that is what my greatest guilt is – I did not report it over human respect, and the fear of being alone.'

34. Flashback: The Murder of a Puppy.

A small stray dog wandered onto the FOB one September day. It was hesitant to approach us, though it was clearly starving. We gave her some goat meat we got from the ANP and the next day she came back. We named her Sheila and for the next couple of weeks, she brought some relief and childlike joy to the Marines. Then the Gunnery Sergeant returned from Camp Bastion.

I was on morning cleaning duty, walking around at first light, picking up plastic bottles, wrappers, and random bits of this and that – a late night sandstorm had fairly distributed trash to all corners of the FOB. Sheila spotted me and ran up to me, jumping around and following me about, requesting attention and play. I did not have time for more than a quick pat. She kept following me as my black garbage bag grew larger and larger. The Gunnery Sergeant emerged from his hooch, and when I saw him, I said:

'Good morning, Gunnery Sergeant!' with the proper courtesy and respect in tone required for his station. Regardless of my opinion of another Marine, I always gave them their due, per regulation.

'Hey, Marine, you see that mangy mutt there?' said the Gunnery Sergeant, with a frown and dead eyes.

'Yes, Gunnery Sergeant. Her name is Sheila.'

'I don't give a fuck what it's called. I want you to get rid of that piece of shit right now. This is a war, not a fucking pet store, and it needs to go.'

'But Gunnery Sergeant, what do you want me to do with her?'

He directed me over to the front ECP gate, opened it, picked up little Sheila by the neck with one arm – she yelped from discomfort – and pointing a knife-hand with his other:

'You see that burn pit over there? Throw the bitch in!' He forced the scared puppy into my arms. I obediently exited the ECP whilst the Gunnery Sergeant closed the gate behind me.

I stopped and hugged the little dog, inducing puppy licks to my face. Slowly, I walked over towards the pit. It was a deep pit, smelling of burning plastic, chemicals, and shit. It was not at full blaze, but there was still a lightly burning tyre on top of a smouldering pile of warped plastic water bottles, trash, human faeces bubbling out of WAG bags, and half burned wooden pallets. Then Sheila stopped licking me and looked at it with curiosity.

Had it been at full blaze, it would surely have been easier to throw the poor puppy into it. Surely then death would be fairly quick, but this – this would be a slow melting and surely screaming. I felt her neck vertebra – I knew how to kill this way. It would be just a quick twist and a snap – no suffering. I stood there and petted her some more whilst thinking. She got tired of being held and wanted down, whimpering when I disallowed her freedom. Looking back towards the ECP, I did not see the Gunnery Sergeant standing on the post or wall. He must have not wanted to hear the sounds of it all and retreated to his hooch.

It would be the only time in my Marine Corps career when I would ever disobey a direct order. I walked over towards the main ECP of the outer wall, which was the ANP territory. I unbolted the gate, and gently placed Sheila outside the FOB, throwing a rock for her to fetch after, and quickly shutting it. As I walked back to our gate, I could hear whimpering and scratching at the metal door. I entered our ECP and walked up to the post, which was manned by Huntly that morning.

'What the fuck, Brodie? What do you think you were doing out there in the ANP zone?! I have to report you, you know!'

'Dude, Gunnery Sergeant ordered me to kill Sheila. He told me to throw her in the burn pit, but I could not do it.'

'That bastard! What the fuck?'

'We need to tell the other Marines not to let her back on the FOB or not only am I getting in trouble – she is going to die.'

'That fucking bastard. Okay, and don't worry, I won't rat you out to anyone either. That's just really fucked. Fucking Mighty Mouse! Fuck that guy...'

After that, we saw Sheila around the town for a little while, always coming up friendly as usual. After a week, she was very skinny. Every time we would see her after that, she had some new injury – a bloody spot, missing fur, torn up ears, then missing an eye. Most dogs in Afghanistan learn from a young age not to approach random people, but we had conditioned her to be friendly to everyone. Afghan people do not treat random dogs like Westerners do. It was normal to see them kick the dogs, throw rocks at them, and shoot them for fun. After a few weeks, we never saw her again. When speaking to Huntly about her disappearance, he told me he thought I should have just snapped her neck. It would have been a less painful death, and I ended up killing her anyways in the long run by letting her outside the wall.

35. Lance Corporal Andrews: Cockfight.

'Man, it sucks all this cartel shit across the border. The Corps won't let us cross anymore.'

'Yeah, I guess. But honestly, I have never really thought about going to Mexico. The culture and history never seemed that interesting, and the food – I mean, we have Taco Bell here.'

'Taco Bell! You serious, man? That shit ain't Mexican! Bro, that's dog food! I'm gonna get you some real shit soon as I get my new leg. You'll see my boy, you're in for a treat!'

'Okay, I guess.'

'But man, we can get good Mexican here in San An. What we can't get anymore, that's in Boy's Town across the border. Used to be we'd drive down on the weekend. You ever seen a donkey show?'

'Donkey show? What is that?'

'Bro, it's when a chick gets railed by a donkey!'

'Are you serious?'

'100% man!'

'That is fucking disgusting. People seriously do that – watch that kind of thing?'

'Hell yeah, bro! Trust me, it's something you gotta see!'

'I do not even watch porn. There is no way I would ever think of seeing something like that.'

'Oh, shit bro? I forgot that you were religious. But shit, man, you really take that shit serious?'

'I do, and even if I did not, I would like to think that I would never participate in something like that.'

'Alright man, I guess I can respect that. So, you'd probably not be down to get a whore either?'

'Absolutely not.'

'Strip clubs?'

'No.'

'Shit man, what can you do for fun then?'

'I like to fish and sometimes have a drink, but I do not do that other stuff.'

'Shit, well I guess there isn't much use of Boy's Town for ya. Wait, what about fights?'

'I enjoy fighting but not much watching it.'

'How's about a dogfight? I know, it's a little fucked up, but they do that down there.'

'I do not know the morality of something like that, but I would say that it is probably not something that is healthy for the human mind to see.'

'Hey, I get that with dogs, but what about birds? Cockfights?'

'Actually, I have seen a cockfight before – in Afghanistan.'

'Oh, hell yeah, man!'

'We used to hire this Afghan National. He was around 16 years old and was somewhat educated – he spoke more English than most of them. He used to cook for us and help with logistics between the ANP and local workers. I was standing post on the one which overlooked the ANP side of the base.'

'I bet you saw some gay shit standing that post?'

'It was not my favourite post – I will say that. Anyways, I saw Ali – the Afghan National – pull two cages out of his car that day. He tossed them to a crowd of ANP and they gave him a bag of drugs. A crowd of them gathered round and they pulled the roosters out of their cages, shaking them, plucking feathers, and smacking them around – making them angry. Then they tossed them at each other as the little crowd cheered. The black cock was larger than the white one and very quickly got at the white cock. The smaller one slashed out with its spurs and some black feathers flew away. But then the larger one jumped up, and sunk its blades into the white bird's chest, ripping it open. It then got round behind it, on top of it, violently pecking at its neck until the feathers turned from white to pink, and then to mostly red.'

'Shit bro, that's brutal shit. I've never seen one before to be honest, but I didn't realise how quick it goes.'

'It was probably less than 30-seconds when the red cock tripped in a failed defensive move, and the black cock got at its face, pecking one of its eyes into a mushy socket. Holding it down, slashing, pecking. The loser attempting to get away but losing more strength. The ANP cheered and Ali walked up, grabbed the victor by its feet with one hand and with the other, he pulled out a rusty machete and quickly sliced off the loser's head. Through the exposed esophagus, the bird's body screamed, gargling on its own fluids. Though decapitated, it got up on its feet and walked back and forth like a drunk at the bar, dripping blood everywhere. Ali put the victor down, which immediately began to attack the headless body until it forced it to the ground and stood over in triumph. As the last twitch of nerves lessened in the body's feet, the ANP went back inside their building, and the killer let out a violent cock-a-doodle-doo three times. Because it had won, it was allowed to live and roam the ANP side of the FOB, and for the remainder of our time in Afghanistan, the creature would sound its victory call every first light.'

'That's fucked, man. I'll be honest, I always thought it might be fun to watch one, but now that you've described it, I don't think it would.'

'Well, I will be honest – I did enjoy it. You get so bored standing post, day after day. It was messed up, but I am not going to lie and say I did not enjoy the blood sport of it.'

'Hey, I get that, man. Post is post. So, about the loser cock? They just leave it there for the black one to eat?'

'Nope. Ali brought it over to mainside, and a little while later, I could smell it roasting in the hut. He brought it over to my post and handed me a cooked wing. Not much meat on it, but it tasted like chicken, and I stood there eating it with him. As he crewed meat off the rib bones and tossed them in the sand, he asked me something I will never forget. He said:'

'What is the fuck?'

'I am sorry, what do you mean?' I replied.

'I hear Marines say the fuck. Marine say fuck good, Marine say fuck bad. They say fuck you and fuck me. What does fuck mean?'

'Well, the word can be used in most contexts, I suppose, I told him. At this Ali looked at me more puzzled and it was clear his English comprehension was not as good as it seemed. And I tried to explain saying: I mean, you can say fuck you, which can be bad, but it can also be a joke. Or you could say fuck this or that, which is bad, but if you say that you want to fuck a girl, that means that she is attractive, I guess. But this may have made him more confused and scratching at his head he asked:'

'I say, my fucking camel, yes?'

'You could say that, yes.'

'But why is? Why Marine say fuck?'

'Umm, I honestly do not know. It is just part of how the language has evolved I guess.'

'Oh! Then, Marine say fuck because Marine don't know why?'

'Yeah, I guess so.'

'Ali then started to practice the word in different forms as he walked back to the hut.'

'Yeah, man, it's funny when ya think about how much we use that word and in how many varieties. It is probably as common as and or but in the Marines. Fuck, it might be more common. But say, you're religious and I hear you say fuck sometimes. Isn't that bad?'

'I suppose I just absorbed the language of the cult slowly, and maybe I never noticed it until I was questioned by him. I suppose stuff like that and how easily it became a normal part of my vocabulary are part of the reason I am so careful about getting involved with stuff like porn and that sort of thing. I am human like everyone else and can easily slip into patterns and behaviour that I do not want to. And possibly without even noticing it, since it would never be questioned in our cult.'

36. The Therapist: Hindu Kush.

'I think it is time for us to get back on track.'

'On track for what?'

'With your therapy. With your prescribed treatment. There are proven methods for treating your disorder, and we—'

'Who says I have a disorder? This stuff that happened to me seems to bother you more than it does me. Maybe you have the disorder?'

'Now, Lance Corporal, that isn't fair, and you know that I am just trying to help you get over what happened to you.'

'Look, I get why some guys need this shit, but, honestly, I am not that bothered. You know, who you should be treating is my friend, Huntly. But he is still on active duty, and I am stuck here. It is really pretty ironic, really. Just because I am visibly fucked up, I get my time wasted by you guys, but the guys who actually need the talks are still working on active duty. It just shows that none of you guys actually care, right? It is just about making money, just another job, right?'

'Now Lance Corporal—'

'Let me tell you about Huntly. Just one of the many things that happened to him.'

'...'

'Our squad had been overwhelmed with patrolling all week, and we just got back from Herat. We had hardly any sleep in days, but our Gunnery Sergeant wanted us to do one more patrol down to Delaram, in Nimruz Province. Our Squad Leader protested this and tried to reason with Gunnery Sergeant. He still said we had to do it but agreed that after we got back that it would be the last patrol we had to do, and we would have the following day off.'

'So, this was your last patrol then? The one where you got blown up!?'

'No. Actually, it was the second to last patrol. Anyways, we mounted up again and traversed through the footstools of the Hindu-Kush Mountain range down to Delaram. The mountains were Taliban territory, but we encountered no resistance. When we reached FOB Delaram, we did whatever we were supposed to do – resupplied, picked up mail, or some shit. One of the things I remember us picking up was a pallet of kids backpacks, each full of basic school supplies, which we loaded onto the seven-ton. We had been helping build schools all over the Western Provinces, and these backpacks were to be given out to local kids to encourage them to go to school.'

'As we exited the FOB and were about to head out of the town, back up into the mountains, the Vics stopped for a few seconds. The Squad Leader was in Vic two and radioed to Vic one what was the hold up. Then there was a boom.'

'Huntly was the gunner of Vic one. A little boy of about seven years old had walked out in front of their Vic, smiling and waving.'

The Therapist scratches their head.

'Huntly should have pointed his gun at the boy and yelled for him to move, or fired a warning flare into the air, or something like that – some EOF. But he saw the boy was wearing a backpack like the ones we had just loaded up, which must have been given to him by the Delaram Marines. This made Huntly happy and feel like all the suffering we had gone through over the last seven months had meant something. All of our brothers who had been killed, had died for something good. Huntly smiled back at the little boy, waved, and gave him a thumbs up. Just then, his backpack exploded, along with him, into pink mist and peppering the Vic with ball bearings.'

The Therapist scratches their head.

'We learned later from the local ANP that the Taliban had bought the boy from his family. His family were by no means Taliban supporters, but they needed the money to survive the coming winter. Two hundred dollars American would be more than enough for their family of 17 to make it well into the spring, and $200 is what they were paid for his life. And the boy knew this too. He kept smiling, knowing his family would survive because of his sacrifice. He kept smiling even as he came apart from himself.'

37. Chaplain Thomas: The Jackal.

'Ah, good afternoon, Lance Corporal Brodie!'

'Good afternoon, sir.'

'Here to see Jeremy, I suspect?'

'Father Jeremy.'

'Indeed.'

'No, actually, I was bored and thought that you might make for some entertainment. Sir.'

'Ha! Well, I must admit, despite your occasional bouts of impertinence, I do find our conversations, as you put it, entertaining. So, what's new? How is therapy going?'

'PT is fine. It hurts, but it is fine.'

'What is it you Marines always say about pain, again?'

'Pain is weakness leaving the body!'

'Ah! That's the one! I suppose that generally falls in line with the idea of spiritual mortification as well. Denying the flesh and all that.'

'Oh, I did not realise your kind still practiced anything at all anymore. Sir.'

'Oh, we try, we do try. And your other therapy, then? How's that going? Last you spoke on it; it sounded like its own form of pain.'

'I still do not like it, but it has not been as bad, I guess.'

'Hmm, you two are coming to a better understanding then?'

'Nope. I just decided to keep playing my own game with it.'

'Indeed. Well, books then? Have you started reading anything?'

'No. I tried but the pain and the medications make it too hard. I cannot retain anything right now.'

'Oh, I'm sorry to hear that. Considering your fascination with old works, I was going to offer you to borrow my copy of the *Complete Works of Charles Dickens.* Have you read him?'

'In high school – I read *A Tale of Two Cities.*'

'Ah, that is one of my favourites! Did you enjoy it?'

'Yes, I did.'

'Which character was your favourite? I always felt like I would have been Mr. Lorry.'

'The Jackal.'

'Really? Why Sydney of all people? I honestly didn't like him, well, until the end at least.'

'I remember reading it and thinking this is me. I am him.'

'Because of his self-sacrifice? I mean you have given a lot for your country, but you said that you read it before the military, right?'

'It was because of her. The same girl. Why I cannot finish the *Iliad*. I never felt that I was good enough for her. It would be better if I died for her sake than lived.'

'Oh, I see. However, you didn't die. You're still here.'

'Better had I died. Look at me, sir. I am now as broken in body as I was broken inside, back then. And that will never change.'

38. Father Jeremy: The Russian Base.

'This one, Father, I am not sure if I sinned or not, but I want to confess it anyways – because – I do not know.'

'We were on the south side of Safarak, near the Rud, test firing the guns on the mountain. The next day, we were joining up with MARSOC to do a raid on Shewan. It was an important raid, and Shewan – it was a really bad area – Taliban held. We had to make sure the guns were all firing good – no stoppages or any of that shit. Oh, excuse me for saying shi— I mean, for saying that, Father.'

'That's okay, Marine. I've heard worse. You can go on.'

'Okay, um, well, so we were testing the guns. I was on the Mark 19 at the time. My Team Leader, Corporal Murphy was the senior gunner, and was normally on the gun, but I had been given it because of his mistake. He was upset with me because of this and wanted to point out my lacking.'

'Hey Boot, I bet ya can't hit the peak!' he said, in a scoff.

'Which peak do you mean, Corporal? The little one nearest our position?'

'Not that little shit. Safarak fucking mountain peak!'

'C'mon, Murph, that's way out of range for the Mark,' said Corporal Diego.

'Remember, intel says there's an old Russian base up there the Taliban use to spy on us from,' said the Squad Leader.

'Yup, I heard they got an old Soviet DShK and a Recoilless rifle up there. At least that's what one of Rambo's victims claimed...,' said Corporal Williams.

'Sure would be a thing if you could hit that peak, Boot,' said Corporal Murphy.

I looked up towards the cathedral tower of the mountain peak. The distance seemed over three miles away, but I remembered when we made the assent of the mountain, because of the structure of it, and how steep it got so quickly and then from that foundation, like daggers, towers rose, I figured there was an element of optical illusion to it. Maybe it was actually under two miles – still out of range. But there was a strong east wind at my back – almost like the overture to a sandstorm. And the memory of how strong the winds were when we slept on that ridge, which was less than a fifth up the mountain. Perhaps the winds up top could be more extreme than that and carry the rounds beyond their natural trajectory.

'Oh, shit, he's going for it!' said Corporal Williams, as I took off the Traversing and Elevation Mechanism. Free handing the Mark 19, I took it to the fullest defilade angle possible in a turret. I fired a six to eight round burst and then a second burst of the same.

We waited. And waited more. After a half a minute, still, no impact, no idea. Impossible. The splash-out from even a single round of 40 millimetre High Explosive Dual Purpose is significant visually and the explosion can be heard for many miles. We were all equally confused. A single dud round is possible, but not two bursts.

'Okay, Boot, what the fuck you do to those rounds?' said Corporal Murphy, but then we all turned. In the distance, from the other side of the mountain, there came the sound of: boom, boom, boom, boom, boom, boom, boom. Then a slight pause, followed by the second volley.

'Fucking shit! Brodie just shot over the fuckin' mountain!' squealed Corporal Williams.

This was amazing – impossible, but true. That had to be nearly four miles away – way beyond the range of the machine gun.

'Well shit, Brodie. If you can make it that far, do you think you could adjust your fire and actually make the peak?' Asked the Squad Leader.

'Yes, Corporal! KILL!'

I adjusted the defilade to account for the wind and supposed distance, and again, fired two six to eight round bursts, and waited. This time, we did not wait long. The first burst impacted around the peak in flashes and the second burst joined and became a cloud of rock fragments. Then the ancient citadel crumbled and fell round itself into the depths. If there was really an old Russian base up there and any Taliban, they were no more. The Marines all cheered at it and even Corporal Murphy came up to me and said:

'Good job, Brodie.'

It was the second time he had ever given me a compliment and the only time he had ever addressed me by my last name.

Then Corporal Williams climbed up to my turret and said: 'What the fuck, Brodie? You trying to put us Mortarmen out of business? Let me have a turn at her?' He turned to the Squad Leader for approval.

'Fine, Brodie, give Williams a shot at it. But Williams, don't you overshoot like Brodie's first shots. There is a little town on the other side of Safarak and we don't need to be raining down HEDP on innocent little boys and girls.'

When the Squad Leader said that it hit me like an electric shock to my spin. I had not thought about the town on the other side. It was good that I had destroyed a potential enemy position, and those two bursts had given me the range information to find it, but it also gave me the estimated location of the initial splash – it must have been close to that village, if not on it. Each round with the individual power to punch through two inches of tank armour, kill anything for sure within five metres of impact, and to wound and potentially kill anyone within 15 metres.

I tried to explain to Corporal Williams as he got in my position about the angle I used, but he did not listen. He fired a long ten or twelve round burst and then a second, both at full defilade. We waited. Like my first shots, no impact, no idea – then the many echoes from the other side.

'What the hell, Williams!?' Yelled up the Squad Leader. 'I told you not to overshoot, mother fucker! There's a fucking town, bro!'

'I know, I know, sorry dude! I'll readjust and try again,' said Corporal Williams.

Then the LT came over the radio, asking for a SitRep. The posts had seen the peak explode and he wanted to know if we were in a firefight. The Squad Leader explained that we were just testing the guns, and the LT got pissed off and told us to return to the FOB.

When we got back to the FOB, Hector and Bo came running up to me, asking what happened. They had been standing post on the main ECP when all of a sudden, the top of Safarak blew up. I told them about it and about how my first bursts went over, and how Corporal Williams' went over – probably landing near the village. They both had the same opinion:

'Who gives a fuck at this point, dude?'

'Yeah, they are probably fucking Taliban or Taliban sympathizers anyways.'

Later that evening, no wounded locals showed up to the FOB for treatment. It was normal for them to come if they got caught in the crossfire or if they had been damaged by the Taliban. The FOB was the only thing close to a hospital in the upper valley and the fact that no one showed up was something of a comfort to me – though I will not lie about it – it bothered me on a moral level – emotionally, I felt nothing.

39. Flashback: Slaughter Night.

One of my last patrols was to support the little ANP outpost East of Shewan. These ANP were pretty incompetent compared to the ones at our FOB. They never reported anything of value and never seemed to arrest anyone – odd considering their proximity to a Taliban held city. This could have been because they were actually Taliban or maybe they were paid off by them, or it could have been the fact that there was a huge Marijuana field with five-foot Cannabis plants just across the street. A lot of the ANP were high all the time on weed or opium, and not much help to anyone.

We pulled up to their outpost that October evening as the sun began to die. Corporal Diego stretched out below and tried to take a nap. Doc was reading a medical book, and I scanned the distance.

Near sunset, I reported seeing a convoy of trucks coming down the hardball from the direction of Highway One towards Shewan. Corporal Diego was woken up by Doc and everyone went on alert. But it was just a convoy of about 50 civilian Jingle Trucks – semi-trucks covered in little bells to ward off evil spirits – approaching the city, heading towards Farah City to trade goods. They knew that the Taliban held the Shewan area, and their convoy included many hired mercenary trucks, armed with AKs. They were encouraged to see us posted up there and there was lots of cheering and thumbs up as they disappeared towards the city.

The last of them had disappeared down the road and into the city. At the darker side of twilight, the first tracers started bouncing, flying off into the skies. Then total violence erupted from the centre of Shewan. It was evident that they had been ambushed by hundreds of Taliban. RPGs exploded in a flash, or missed, skipped off and landing in a flash against some wall or in the street. The sound from it was delayed and it was eerie like the sea when it came.

I got excited and racked the Mark 19, expecting to be ordered to engage soon, but then the Squad Leader radioed to stand down. He radioed the LT with a SitRep. The LT would then radio Command at Camp Bastion. Whilst we waited for word, the violence continued.

'This is bullshit, Doc! They are getting slaughtered out there! And because of bureaucratic paperwork, we are just sitting here doing nothing.'

'I know, but that is the way the system is, Brodie.'

'It is fucking bullshit! Civilians are being killed right in front of us and we are here, loaded, and ready to fight. We are Marines and we are just sitting here watching.'

'We aren't going to fight, Brodie,' said Corporal Diego.

'What do you mean, Corporal?'

'It's simple. We're combat inefficient. The Taliban know it and that's why they are fucking those guys up. They know we won't do a thing about it. And we haven't had air on station in weeks. Without air support, there is no way they'd let us attack.'

'But what is the point then, Corporal? Why are we even here if we cannot do anything.'

'Fuck if I know, Marine. Fuck if I know.'

Darkness came and fires grew throughout the city, explosions continued, AK and machine gunfire continued. After around 30-minutes, the last tracer ricocheted up and disappeared into the skies, signalling the death of the last defender. Around this time, Command got back to the LT and then to our Squad Leader. The order was to stand down, remain vigilant, and to observe. There was no air support available, no backup, no support advised. It was too late anyways, but it still hurt – all those people slaughtered.

In the morning, you could see black smoke for miles from the many burning tyres.

40. Lance Corporal Andrews: Standing Post.

'Man, you know what I miss most about the Middle East?

'What is that?'

'That bread. That shit is good. Can't find that in San Antone.'

'Agreed. That was good stuff. Even after I found out how they make it, I still kept eating it. It was that good.'

'What ya mean by that?'

'You know, the fuel they use to make it. I know it is nasty, but I still kept eating.'

'I never seen 'em make it. What's this fuel thing about?'

'Well, there is a reason why we call it shit bread.'

'What the?'

'Yup, they cook it over dried human faeces.'

'Fuck? You kidding me, dude?'

'Nope, it is the truth. Well, I do not know about the stuff you had in Iraq, to be fair, but in Farah Province, there are not many trees. They use what they have to cook. They have big piles of it drying against the walls outside where they cook. In fact, I remember once we did a foot patrol at night, and we stopped in a courtyard and set up a cordon. When it was my turn to sleep, I found a nice incline on the wall. When I was woken up in the first morning light, I noticed what that incline was made of.'

'Shit, man. That's fucked. I think the Iraqis had better resources than that. Can't say I've heard or seen that shit. To be honest bro, it sounds like Afghan was much wilder than Iraq. Hell, half what I did on my second deployment was just stand post.'

'Oh, I stood plenty of post too. You have a lot of thinking time while you are standing up there, looking out into the desert.'

'Just don't lean against the wall, if you know what I mean.'

'Yup, the number of guys standing that same spot, 10 hours at a time, often in the dark.'

'Ya know, I kinda miss standing a night post. Seeing the sun set and then rise. So damn wholesome.'

'Yeah, agreed. Except when I got woken up for them in the middle of the night, I generally liked a night watch.'

'The heat ain't half bad at night either.'

'Near the end of September, it started getting pretty nice out too.'

'Yip.'

'I remember one night; I was scanning the desert – it was at the darker side of twilight – I thought I saw something approaching the FOB a mile out.'

'Talibans?'

'Nope, but my heart began to beat, hoping it was. I picked up my rifle and looking through the ACOG, I tried making it out. The crescent moon had climbed over the western mountains, glazing the sand. I could not see it well, but it looked like a man, crawling towards me. I called it in on the radio, and Corporal Diego came running up with the thermal binoculars.'

'You see something, Brodie?'

'About a mile out, left of the river, right of the broken wall.'

'Got it! Hahaha, good eyes, Marine! Here take a look.'

'Is that a cat?'

'You ever hear a strange sound at night? A sound like a retard laughing?'

'Yes, I have. It always freaks me out.'

'That's the little bastard that makes the sound. It's a Desert fox. Good eyes, Marine, good looking out. Keep the thermals for now, and radio me again if you see a human heat signature.'

'I watched the little fox as it approached the FOB. It looked up at the Hesco wall and then jumped up it. I saw the heat from its little paw come over the edge of the wall and then it jumped over, and stood on the wall, looking directly at me. I put the thermals down to see it in the moonlight. It stayed, looking at me. Then licked its front paws, jumped down, and disappeared into the FOB. I did not see it again for nearly a month. Then, the night before our last patrol, I saw it again. That time, it stopped a little longer, looking at me in the moonlight.'

41. The Therapist: Mighty Mouse.

'Now, Lance Corporal Brodie. I may be your therapist, but I am also an Army Major. I'm an officer, and if I order you to do something, you are required to do it!'

'Not quite. You see, you are Army, I am Marines, but also, I am an Infantry Marine. You are just a POG and have no right to tell the Infantry what to do. You have no authority over me, and in the Warrior Class structure, you are beneath me in honour and respect.'

'Now listen to me, Lance Corporal!'

'No, listen to me, Therapist! That is your job, anyways. You think that you know everything – you know, you remind me of our Gunnery Sergeant sometimes. We called him Mighty Mouse. Partly because of his structure, partly because of how pumped up full of shit he was. Really, he was just an incompetent POG, who somehow got in charge of our platoon. He treated us with no respect, overworked us, had gotten two Marines killed already, and even got our puppy killed. Finally, everyone had enough, and there was a meeting between most of the FOB about killing him.'

The Therapist scratches their head.

'All of the Seniors were on board with it, and most of the Boots were either silent, or verbally agreed.'

'We should frag that motherfucker!' said Chad.

'Huntly agreed. Both Hector and I were silent at first, but then Hector also agreed. Doc Ramos was silent, but he did not protest. I was very conflicted. On the one hand, I was a practicing Catholic, and thought it was very wrong. But – I agreed with the general consensus: this guy was going to get us killed. I was surprised to hear Corporal Diego join in on the plan for how it would be done. I was not surprised that Corporal Murphy was one of the leading drafters of the plan. They were going to draw straws and on one of the nights when the LT and other higher ups were back at Camp Bastion for resupply, the one who drew the short straw would toss a grenade into the Gunnery Sergeant's tent. I thought about it a lot. And in the end, I decided that I would remain silent – not contribute to the plan, but also not report it to the higher ups. Besides, if I did report it, they would just frag me as well. If not that, I would be a traitor, and an outcast again.'

'It never happened, though. In the end, someone else must have snitched to the higher ups. We knew because the next morning, we were all woken up by the higher ups, who went from Marine to Marine, confiscating all of our frags. From then on, we would only be given them when we were about to go on post or patrol.'

'Well, that's probably for the best. You could—'

'No – I do not know about that. I mean, my Marines would not be dead, and I would not be a cripple now, were it not for him.'

The Therapist scratches their head.

'Anyways, after that, one of the Marines caught a mouse and killed it. They made a little noose which they hung it from, over the opening of the Gunnery Sergeant's tent. They superglued a little cardboard sign to its paws, on which was written: Mighty Mouse is Dead. After that, he stopped going out on patrols with us and stayed on the mainside of the FOB.'

42. Chaplain Thomas: Damages.

'Good afternoon, Marine. How are we doing today?'

'Good afternoon, sir. I am just on my way to see orthopaedics. What are you up to in the hospital today?'

'Oh, you know, typical Protestant business.'

'Oh, sir, but there are not any puppies for you to drown here.'

'Ha! So, what's going on with ortho?'

'I am going to ask them for another amputation. I am tired of the pain, the drugs, and all the pointless therapy. I just want to be over with it.'

'Ah, well that is a very hard choice, but I suppose I get what you mean. I've only been stationed here for two years, and in that time, I've seen many young men make similar decisions. How are you doing with the idea of it?'

'Like I said, sir, I just want it to be done and over with. Just cut it off and let me get on with my miserable life.'

'Don't you think it might be less miserable after it. I mean as far as the pain and mobility?'

'I do not care at this point. I just want it to be over.'

43. Father Jeremy: Kill Bodies.

'I have another thing I would like to confess as well, Father.'

'Alright, go ahead, when you are ready.'

'Towards the end of the deployment, I started getting angry with God.'

'Angry because of your friends getting hurt?'

'No. Because I wanted to see more action – more combat and I knew He was keeping me from it. Most of the other gunners had been in proper firefights more than once at that point. Sure, I had been shot at quite a bit and had shot at people too, but I did not have a confirmed kill – I just wanted more. More war. A lot of Marines are like this, but I wanted it more than most.'

'And why do you think God was keeping you from it?'

'I know why. It is because I wanted it so much and He knows me. If He gave it to me, I would only want more, and more – I would have never left the Marines. Never left Afghanistan. I did not want to leave. Most of the other guys wanted to go home and see their families. I did not care about mine anymore. I had already stopped calling them – whenever my turn with the satellite phone came up, I always gave up my 30-minutes to one of the married Marines. They thought it was because I was a good Catholic boy, but really – I did not want to talk to anyone back home anymore. It was not my home anymore, Afghanistan was, and the Marines were my family – in a way, so was the Taliban.'

'Hmm, well. Well, I suppose I can understand what you mean. That that is not what God would want for you, but still, I don't know why that would make you angry at him?'

'There were times when it was obvious that he was intervening – keeping me from the bloodiest fights. The time that things got quiet for a month. Chad and I both wanted more action, so we volunteered as PSD Upgunners to Bakwa for a few days. The moment we arrived in Bakwa, on the other side of the mountain range, my squad got into one of the biggest firefights on the deployment. Huntly got the Navy Cross. It was also why I got put on the Mark 19. Corporal Murphy froze in the firefight and was unable to clear the gun when it jammed. And Corporal Williams had been put on the 50 cal that day – my gun at the time. It jammed too and he could not clear it. I would have cleared it! I would have laid down both suppressive fire and I would have cut them to pieces! Instead, I listened to it on the green gear from Bakwa.'

'Well, I don't think you can blame God for that. It is war and things happen unexpectedly. Also, you volunteered for that mission. Do you not think that maybe He was going to give you what you wanted, but because you didn't trust him, you went your own way instead?'

'I think he let my Guardian Angel give me the inclination to volunteer for that so I would not be there.'

'And why is that?'

'Had I been there, the 50 would have been blazing, and all of the enemy attention would have been on me. I would have died that day – a glorious death in combat! And He did not want that for me. That makes me angry, because I wanted that honour more than anything else.'

'I see.'

'It was not just that day, Father. There were so many times like that. There were times when I should have been on a patrol, but another

Senior wanted my gun that day. There were times when I should have been on a raid, and I was put on post duty instead. There was a time – one of the most upsetting ones – when I should have been one of the main gunners in a big fight, and as we were leaving the FOB, our truck engine started smoking randomly – that never happens. They made my Vic stay back for that. That was the only time I cried on deployment. I went back to the tent and cried because I was denied what I was trained for and wanted.'

'God has a plan for everyone.'

'I know, Father, and I believe that. I do. But that, the war, it was all taken away from me. And because of the severity of my injuries, I will never be allowed to go back. It is all gone now, forever, and there is nothing left for me.'

44. Flashback: Kill Babies.

On Highway One, patrolling the mountain pass between Farah Rud and Delaram, we came across an unusual amount of traffic for that bit of road. They seemed to be backed up for miles and only recently began to move. I looked into the windows as we drove past. There were whole families stuffed into small cars and men driving Jingle Trucks. There were young people with their heads turned away or eyes down, or, looking intently back at you – the Taliban or Taliban sympathizers. There were young people who waved, gave thumbs up, and smiled. There was an old man holding two goats on his lap. There was a charred man with no face sitting next to a young man who beckoned to me. The shock of the sight hit me. I was not sure if I had hallucinated what I had just seen. Then I heard on the radio from the Vic behind me:

'Hey, Squad Leader, this is Vic four – over. There is some guy with no face and burned all over back here – over. He needs medical attention – over.'

'Roger that. Vic four. All Vics hold up – over. Vic three, Vic three, dismount with Vic four and have Doc take a look – over. I'll bring the Terp – over.'

The burn victim had been picked up by some charitable Afghans traveling to Herat. They had found him lying over an IED hole just up the mountain pass and were taking him to us for medical attention. From what the Terp gathered, it was apparent that the guy was a Taliban who had been setting an IED for our patrol to hit today, but he had set it off in the process, injuring himself. The ANP wanted us to just leave him by the side of the road and let him die in the sun, but we decided to end the patrol early and take him back for treatment.

On the way back, we forced all of the traffic out of the way, and this pissed off one of the civilian vehicles that sped around Vic four, trying to pass the patrol. Corporal Murphy had been moved to the turret of Vic four after the incident with the Mark 19, and he quickly fired a flare at the car to warn them. The flare pierced through the windshield and the Vic stopped. A team of Marines dismounted to check the car. The driver was a very impatient husband taking his wife to Herat to see a doctor. She was sitting in the back seat, unconscious. When the flare went through, it hit her in the face, breaking her jaw.

She was loaded by her husband into the empty seat of my Vic and again we continued towards the FOB. When we arrived, both of the injured Afghans were taken to the medical shack. An hour later, we were able to get a medevac for them. Several of us, including Doc Ramos and myself helped carry the two of them on stretchers to where the Dutch helo would land. While we waited for it to land, I looked down and saw her face. I had never been this close to an Afghan woman and never seen one's face. Her jaw was wrapped up with gauze and medical tape, soaked red. Her eyes were closed, and she moaned from pain and morphine. She had a pierced nose, many ear piercings, and some small, strange tattoos on the side of her face and near her eyes. She might have been in her 30s, but possibly much younger. It was hard to tell with Afghans, as they had such harsh lives and aged so much quicker in the desert sun. Her dress was wet with blood at and below the hip. The burned Taliban said something to her and grabbed at her face with a skeletal claw. He was brushed away by Doc Ramos, who told him to leave her alone. He resisted and was held down until we were able to load him on the bird.

After the helo had taken off and we had gone to the medical shack to wash the blood off our hands from moving them, I asked Doc why she was so bloody so low on her body if only her jaw was broken. He told me that the stress from being hit with the flare had caused her body to miscarry the baby she carried in her womb.

45. Lance Corporal Andrews: COMPLACENCY KILLS!

'Hey man, you never told me how you got blown up.'

'Yeah.'

'Shit, man, have a Newport.'

'Thanks.'

'I mean, ya don't have to tell me about it if you don't want to. I was just curious and ya know, sometimes it helps gettin' things off your chest, ya know.'

'I can tell you, if you like. It is long, and there were a lot of reasons, really.'

'Yeah man! Go for it, bro! I'm all ears.'

'Corporal Williams had been made my driver after several fuckups. Despite Corporal Williams' complacent attitude, I always kind of liked him, but he could be a real dumbass sometimes. Like one time, we were driving back from Farah and driving through a chokepoint in the desert. He kept messing with me, grabbing at my legs, and poking me in the butt. Then he picked up a rusty screwdriver and started poking me really hard with it. I asked him to cut it out and so did Doc Ramos. Corporal Diego thought it was funny and just laughed. He just kept poking at me and poking at me, and then – BOOM! An IED blew up on the Vic in front of us. It was not a big IED, and just took out one of the tyres. I squatted down in my turret and yelled at him: THIS IS WHAT HAPPENS WHEN YOU FUCK AROUND! I was still a PFC and obviously had no business speaking to an NCO like that, but he acknowledged he had should have been doing his job. He should have had his eyes on the road, and he was distracting me from the same. Not that it would have helped in this situation, but you know what we always say in the Infantry.'

'Yip! Complacency kills!'

'Exactly. Marines start fucking around near the end of deployments because they get too comfortable, too proud, and too selfish.'

'Seen it myself, brother.'

'Anyways, it was near the very end of our deployment. I had just picked up Lance Corporal. Our squad was finishing up a week of long patrols. We had just done one to Farah, followed by one to Herat, and both on no sleep – I think we had gone three days without sleep by the time we got back to the FOB. We should have been given a rest, but the Gunnery Sergeant came up when we got in and said we had to do one more drive to Delaram. Our Squad Leader tried to reason with him on this, asking for another squad to take it, or to at least give us a couple of hours sleep before. The Gunnery Sergeant said no, but did say that after we did it, another squad would take the rest of the patrols for the week. And he promised us a full night's sleep on our return. None of us had had more than four hours a night in months, so the incentive of this raised our spirits some.'

'Fuck that, man! That's fucked! They can't have Marines on no sleep driving all over the fucking country and expect them to be effective killers.'

'Agreed, but we did it. We went to Delaram. It turned out he sent us there, just to pick up his mail – we were only there about twenty minutes before we mounted up again and did the long drive back. Normally, we would go slow, to look for IEDs, and the drive should take four hours. We did it in two that day, at the Squad Leader's orders. We got back to Farah Rud, unloaded the Vics in the FOB, and went straight to our racks. I will never forget that moment. Like the rest of the guys, I was sitting on my cot, taking off my boots, ready to collapse into the rack, when the Squad Leader came in. He told us to all stop what we were doing and pay attention.'

'Marines, keep your boots on. I am very sorry to have to say it, but we have to do another patrol.'

We all burst into laughter – a stupid joke, but we were so sleep deprived and it was so ridiculous.

'Damn it, Marines! I'm serious! Fucking Mighty Mouse says someone needs to show the Army National Guard around the area, and 1st Squad, or 2nd was supposed to do it, but since both of their Squad Leaders are Sergeants and I'm Corporal, I was overruled.'

'That is fucking bullshit!' was the consensus.

'I know, I know. But my hands are tied. Listen Marines, the Gunnery Sergeant promises, if we do this, it will be our squad's last patrol of the deployment. No more patrols, just standing post, QRF, and relaxing.'

'Where is the patrol to?' asked Corporal Diego.

'The ANP post across from the pot field.'

'You mean the one near fuckin' Shewan?' said Corporal Murphy.

'Hold up, fucking Mighty Mouse wants us to do a patrol, on no sleep, in the fucking dark, near that fucking place?' said Corporal Diego.

'Wouldn't it be better to take the Army guys there tomorrow, in the daylight, so they could actually see that area? They won't be able to see anything tonight,' said Doc Ramos.

'Listen gents, I get it, I get it. I already said all this to fucking Mighty Mouse, but he gave me an order.'

'Doc Ramos was usually the rear passenger in my Vic, but that night Corporal Murphy wanted him in his, and they put an Army Specialist in his seat. The Army National Guard had shown up a week before and I did not know any of them. I chatted to this one a little whilst we waited to leave – he had a new baby waiting at home and seemed like a pretty decent guy, for a Soldier.'

'We drove out to the ANP post and introduced the Army to the ANP and area – though you could not see much in the dark. After an hour, we started to head back. Corporal Williams had fallen asleep and had to be kicked awake – he should not have been driving. None of them should have really. The Squad Leader came over the radio saying that we were going to increase our speed in order to get back sooner. You know the rules – we were supposed to keep our speed under 30mph at night, so we could spot IEDs, and a lower rate of speed causes less pressure and less chance of setting one off a pressure plate. We increased speed above 60.'

'At 21:27, I checked my radio for the last time. I was trying my best to stay awake and to look for IEDs, but with only my NVG monocle, at that rate of speed, there was nothing to see. I stood, holding the grip on the Mark 19, but even standing, I started to fade out. I started thinking to myself: if I fell asleep, it would not make a difference. Then I had a strange dream that a dark angel took me up into the air and then threw me down to the earth, and everything got very warm.'

'Lieutenant Joseph was the CO at Bakwa, on the other side of the mountain range. He recently told me in a Facebook message that the explosion was so extremely large, that they could see the firelight from Bakwa, like it was a lightning bolt.'

46. The Therapist: Last Patrol/The Confrontation.

'We have known each other for a while now.'

'Yes.'

'Are you ready to talk about that night?'

I scratch at my head. 'Which night?'

'The night of your accident.'

'It was not an accident. They knew what they were doing when they made the bomb, dug the hole. It was deliberate. It was successful. Good job, Taliban.'

'I'm sorry, so not accident—'

'No, if anything I cannot blame them.'

'Blame them? The Taliban?'

'Yes, I cannot hold it against them. I hold no hatred for them. I mean, I wish they had not killed my friends and made me a cripple, and I think that an IED is a very dishonourable way to attack someone, but so is dropping bombs from the sky. Not that we had air support very often, but when we did, we dropped them. It is not like they ever had the option of air, so they dug holes instead.'

'Interesting. So, you have nothing against them? No rage, no anger?'

'No. I do not agree with their cause, but I understand their perspective. They see how fucked up the West has become, and their best equation against this is to go backwards in time. I do not agree with how they carry it out, their rules, especially their treatment of women in general. However, I do understand them. In the end, they do not want a country of a bunch of lazy, depressed, apathetic, and utterly worthless individuals – this is most of the West. This is why I joined the Marine Corps. I looked around and I saw the average teenage male in High school, and I said: enough. I do not want to be one of these. I want to be more. I do not want to be just another man-child.'

'You can't just judge an entire generation of Americans like that—'

'Yes, yes, I can. I am an Alaskan. The average Alaskan 10-year-old girl – like my little sister – she can catch a salmon, gut it, and cook it herself. She can load a gun, fire it with effect, and then clean it. Chop down a tree, build a fire, make warmth. All these young men in school, when they are hungry, they whine to their mothers to make them food or their fathers for spending money. They rely on the system for their security. Someone else to take care of their problems. That is why I joined. The honour in that. Not being one of them, and at the same, I would take their burden for them.'

'It sounds like you have more animosity for young Americans than for the Taliban who hurt you?'

'I would not say that. Rather, I respect the Taliban more than them. You see, the Taliban gave me a war. And a war is all that an Infantry Marine wants. In this, the Taliban and I share more brotherhood than I do with the American. At least they served their function.'

'Well, you know, I think, that despite all of that, what you need to get out is that night. I think you're suffering from survivor's guilt and—'

'Survivor's guilt? Are you fucking retarded? No, you know what I am suffering from, aside from having to listen to you go on and on with your typical civilian assumptions about what it is like and what is wrong with war veterans – what is wrong with me is I did not get enough war. I am a cripple now and forever. And I will never get to be on the front line again. Let alone be a real Marine again. To quote Pinocchio: I just want to be a real boy.'

'Okay, I understand what you mean about your loss, but—'

'Do you read?'

'Ah, well, yes I—'

'Have you ever read Hemingway?'

'Ye—'

'Ernest Hemingway?'

'Yes, I have read—'

'Good! Then you may know some of his famous quotes?'

'Well, I can't—'

'My favourite one goes like this: There is no hunting like hunting of man, and those who have hunted armed men long enough and liked it, never care for anything else thereafter.'

47. Chaplain Thomas: Done/Loss.

'You are a hard one to find these days!'

'Good afternoon, sir.'

'Good afternoon, Lance Corporal. How are we doing today?'

'I do not know. Sir.'

'Is there something wrong? Something I can help with?'

'There is plenty wrong, but none of it can be helped. They are going to cut it off finally.'

'Oh, but isn't that something you wanted?'

'Yes, but now that it is going to happen, it feels so strange. Just a couple of months ago, I was a strong and powerful Marine, and now I am a cripple for life. And it seems like they just keep cutting more of me away. Am I even a real person anymore?'

'Of course, you are, Marine.'

'And if I am, does it matter? Is a limb part of a person? Is it part of what makes them, them?'

'Well, in a way, I suppose.'

'If it does, then I am less of a person now, or at least less of myself. And about to become even less myself.'

'Now, Lance Corporal. You talk like all hope is lost. You have your faith still.'

'I do, sir. I have my faith. But I know now, for sure – she will never love me again.'

48. Father Jeremy: The Dead.

'Hi, Father.'

'Hello, Marine! How are you doing today?'

'They confirmed the amputation, Father. It is tomorrow. I was hoping to have a Confession before. Just in case I do not wake up from it.'

'Oh, well, yes, of course. And you will surely be in my prayers as well... we'll have a mass said for you too. What is it you wanted to discuss?'

'I do not feel any guilt about surviving the explosion.'

'Well, that isn't a sin. If anything, it is a good thing.'

'Maybe, Father, but I think somehow, I should have guilt, or maybe other people make me feel like I should. It was not my fault. I was the Upgunner in the turret. Statistically, I was the most likely to die. It was at night. Part of my job was to look for IEDs, but our Squad Leader had ordered that we go at 60mph, rather than the rule. There was no way I could have seen it at that speed, especially at night. Maybe if the truck was not so overloaded with extra 40mm grenades, rockets, and fuel – maybe the extra weight is what set it off. Maybe the explosion would have been smaller. But that was the LT's call. He made me overload the truck. And Corporal Williams, he was driving. He was tired, we all were – we should have never been given that patrol in our state. But Corporal Williams, he knew better. He should have swerved, like the Vic in front of him did, when they saw the repaved spot in the hardball. Frankly, Corporal Diego should have yelled at him to swerve. He was a great Marine, but he, like most of the Seniors, had become complacent at the end of the deployment. He was asleep. I am glad he was too. The pain was probably less because of it.'

'Well, I can see why you wouldn't have guilt about it given all that. It sounds like you were the victim to others' folly.'

'I do not have guilt, but – I do. Throughout my whole deployment, I never sat on the gunner's strap, I always stood. I was very proud of that. It was the reason I was the best Upgunner. I was always alert, and it is harder to fall asleep whilst standing. That night though, I remember leaning against the gun for some support. The exhaustion had caught up and I hungered for sleep. I remember thinking: what is the point? We are going too fast for me to see an IED. It is the last patrol of the deployment. What does it matter if I fall asleep now? Then, I think I did, and at that moment of consent, we hit the bomb. I think God had always protected my truck in the past because of my honour, but when I lost it in that act of consent, I lost His protection, and we blew up. There are no coincidences.'

49. Flashback: The Explosion.

I – I could not hear anything. It was very bright; the desert was lit up all around me from different fires. I felt very hot and when I tried to inhale, it was difficult – painful to breathe. I was in my turret, standing and leaning on the Mark 19, and now I was on my back in the sand, looking out into the dark from so many fires. It was so hot – the October night and the speed of the truck against the air was rather cold. Now I was hot. I looked down at my legs and they were on fire. I wondered what sort of strange dream I was having. Then I looked into one of the fires off to the right of me – maybe five yards away. A body – a human body was burning. I started hearing a long ringing sound in my ears and then from a smoking radio in the sand I could hear someone yelling:

'IED! IED! Vic three just hit an IED!'

I looked at the body in the fire, as the realisation of what was going on came more into reality. It was Corporal Diego. I tried standing up and heard and felt an internal crunch – the pain of my femur snapping was like nothing else since. I started crawling towards him, wanting to put his fire out – the pain was so bad I closed my eyes for a moment. When I opened them, I looked at his face. His eyes were melting into him, as was the rest of his face. It was hopeless then, and I turned to my own injuries.

The fire had begun to burn deep into my meat, and I was now becoming more conscious of the severity of what was going on. I thought about doing the whole stop, drop and roll thing, but it was too painful a motion. With both of my gloved hands, I patted the fire out on the right leg first, which burned with less intensity and only up to my knee. It hurt to press on the burned skin and broken bones, but I endured it. Then I moved to the left leg. The fire had now eaten up into my thigh bone. It burned through the edges and holes in my glove as I pressed against my burning flesh. The hardest part to put out was below the knee, because of the compound fractures – my tibia and fibula bone stuck out of my leg near the ankle – one looked like the ember of a freshly lit cigar. The other burned like a lit Zippo lighter with too long a wick. I had to do it. I put them out and then laid down, gripping the sand in pain. The thigh was still smoking and was so hot that by the time I leaned back up, it had reignited from the heat. I put it out again.

A rocket shot out into the desert and exploded the dark to light. I could hear many other explosions going on around me. I was sure that the Taliban had ambushed us. I looked around for my rifle, but it was nowhere I could see. I checked for my bayonet, but that was stowed in my turret. I felt the front pocket of my flak jacket for my KA-BAR knife – it must have been dislodged when I flew up into the air. Then I felt for my frag. The grenade was there, and it was so hot from the explosion that it burned my already burned hands. It was my only weapon now and it was so hot, it could easily cook off and explode on its own at any second.

I had an important decision to make then regarding honour and morality. I could feel a faintness coming on and thought I might pass out soon. No Marine had ever been captured in Iraq or Afghanistan – the Army had had Soldiers captured, but not us. I was not about to be the one to disgrace my Corps. I could either pull the pin on the frag myself right then, take myself out honourably, and be done with it. Or I could try to stay conscious and at least take some of them out with me, when they came for me. Also, I was pretty sure I was going to die soon anyways – every breath was a struggle. And then there was the moral issue – suicide is always wrong. I had been blown up and out very many yards into the desert, and all I could see was fire, explosions, and the dark – no other Marines, but for Corporal Diego – his fire had now burned him down and charred like a forgotten piece of meat on a BBQ pit. I pulled the pin slowly from the grenade, keeping a firm grip on the safety level, but then pushed it back in. I remembered my training. I felt faint – why? I had not checked for blood.

I looked down and saw the sand was coloured red and wet underneath me. I felt around, looking for the source of the leak, and found I was bleeding from both legs in different places. I felt for my Med kit and got out the tourniquet. My secondary tourniquet was stowed with my bayonet in the turret, so I only had this one. I decided the left leg was the worse of the two and started turning down the windless – tightening it around my thigh. The pain was unbearable, and I nearly fainted from it. I readjusted it as high as I could into my crotch, tightened it until it would go no more.

Then, out from the dark, Chad and Huntly came running towards me. I let out what sound I could, and they found me.

50. Lance Corporal Andrews: The End.

'You know, I wish you could have seen my feet, when I had them. I had big hairy Hobbit feet. I used to love the feeling of sinking them into the sand of the river. But that is gone now.'

'Fuck man, I'm sorry. I mean, I kind of get what you are saying, but I still have one foot.'

'You know, something I keep thinking about.'

'What's that?'

'Well, you know, one of my legs got blown off in Afghan. Basically, crusty mush, was all that was left. But the right leg got amputated here. They tried to do limb salvage. It failed. And just last week they – yeah.'

'Yeah, I'm sorry, brother—'

'No, no, it is alright. I accept it. What I keep thinking about. The leg that was blown off and burned up, when that happened, I had not been to Confession in seven months. When I had the right leg amputated here, I had gone to Confession.'

'You have to remember, brother, I was raised Southern Baptist. I don't really understand what you mean.'

'Well, basically, when the left leg went, I was in a state of sin. When the right leg was cut off, I was in a State of Grace.'

'Okay. I sort of get it.'

'So, if you die in a State of Grace, you go to Heaven, state of sin, hell.'

'Yeah, sure.'

'Well, now, does that mean my left leg is in hell right now? And my right leg in Heaven? Now hear me out, if that is the case, regardless of if I go to either one, one of them should be in the other place, right?'

'Huh, that's kinda fucked up, if it works that way.'

'I know, right. And if it does work that way, I am still going need a prosthetic leg, in either place...'

The Epilogue: Safarak and back

July 4th, 2008, but there would be no Independence Day celebrations for our squad, save only one lonely red star cluster later that evening.

The LT had decided that we needed to climb Mount Safarak to rule out the possibility of the old Soviet base up there being occupied and in use by the Taliban. This was of course before I blew up the top of the mountain months later. The ANP insisted that the Taliban had a Recoilless rifle and a DShK up there and that the mountain was well garrisoned. ANP reports had by now become less and less reliable, but Command decided that the mountain needed to be properly surveyed on foot. The one aerial scan that had been afforded us was inconclusive because of the extreme heat, and they would not offer us any further air support towards further inspection. Most of the air was still at work in Iraq and Afghanistan was not being taken very serious at all by the Pentagon.

Our mission would be to climb Safarak whilst fully armed and to expect resistance – snipers, machine guns, maybe even close quarters and bayonets. We were to assess the mountain for defensive positions, locate the Russian base, and destroy any enemies, weapons, and positions. We would have no QRF, save that 2nd Squad would ascent the mountain from a different spot, with the intention of one squad being able to back up the other. We did not have enough Corpsmen for both Squads, so Doc Ramos went with the larger element from 2nd Squad.

Our team comprised of the Squad Leader, Corporal Diego, Corporal Murphy, Corporal Williams, Chad, Huntly, and me. We were issued no climbing gear at all – no ropes or anything at all. And aside from myself, no one had any experience in climbing, save for the Boot Camp obstacle course.

'Why the hell do we have to put on camouflage face paint for this shit? It's gonna be hot enough and there's no point anyways. That shit is for boots,' said Corporal Williams.

'I agree. This is some horse shit,' said Corporal Diego.

'Look gents, I get it, but the LT thinks it will help us blend into the rocks as we climb and protect us from sniper fire,' said the Squad Leader.

'Fuckin' tarded ass, Lieutenant,' said Corporal Murphy. 'He wants to keep us safe from sniper fire then why the fuck he sending us up there? It's all fucking tarded.'

All the same, we followed orders and began to apply the paint. I helped Doc Ramos with his paint and waited for him to help with mine.

'What the fuck you fags doing? This ain't makeup, put it on like man,' said Corporal Murphy, spiting tobacco spit on the ground and then digging his fingers into his paint, and applying it liberally over his face without use of the small mirror in the case.

The temperature rose to 115-degree Fahrenheit as the trucks approached the base of the mountain and our two groups were separated. I had never been this close to the base of Safarak, and as we neared, and looking up, what had seemed difficult, but doable from the FOB now looked incredibly daunting. Clearly, the LT had never seen the base of the mountain nor had any significant reconnaissance been made – and if it had been, it surely had not been analysed correctly. Further to this, the fact that this particular location was picked for ascent, rather than one of the very obviously less dangerous points confused me. I understood that not everyone had experience with climbing, but surely Command should have noticed that the only way up without climb gear was a small and very steep gully, which was not defensible – one half decent sniper could easily pick us off without any repercussions at all. Even if we had air support, any counterattack at all would cause the mountainside to fall on us. I thought to myself: Are they really serious? Is the Marine Corps truly this incompetent? Are we all going to die today and for nothing?

Corporal Murphy noticing my look of thought spit out his old dip on the rocks and said: 'Yup, Boot, we're fucked.'

'Alright, Marines, let's get up there,' said the Squad Leader.

'It'll be alright, gents. Let's just get up as high as we can without falling or catching a bullet and get through the night,' said Corporal Diego.

'Fuck, man, this is fucking gay, bro,' said Corporal Williams.

Chad, Huntly, and I remained silent and began the climb.

After about 30-minutes of labour, the Squad Leader told us to halt, take off our helmets, and strap them to our packs. We were sweating so much, and the camo paint was mixing with our sweat and getting in our eyes. All of the patterns written on our faces had melted and we looked like we had stuck our faces into the mud.

We continued up another half an hour, every minute, every step, getting steeper, harder going, less options for cover, more exposed. At 200 feet, we halted because we heard a load sound. Corporal Williams had not properly affixed his helmet to his pack and it had come loose, hit against the rock, and fell, rolled, knocking against the rock all the way to the bottom of the mountain.

'You stupid fucking idiot, Williams!' said the Squad Leader.

'Are you actually retarded, Williams?' said Corporal Diego.

'I'm sorry, guys! I—' replied Corporal Williams before being interrupted by Corporal Murphy.

'You were a shitbag in Iraq and ain't improved at all. The fuckin' Boots are less of dumb shits than you, Williams.'

'Well Williams, you gonna climb back down there and get it?' said the Squad Leader.

'Shit man, I'm too fucking tired for that.'

'You're such a fat piece of shit, Williams. You should have joined the Army with the rest of the fatasses, you walrus fuck,' said Corporal Diego.

I was a bit shocked by this. Corporal Diego was generally very kind to people – even ones who did not deserved it – but he was really giving it to Corporal Williams.

Despite the danger of a Marine without a helmet in case of an attack, the Squad Leader agreed that it was unrealistic at this point to go back down for it. We would not have time to ascend to a more defensible area and climbing in the dark would be impossible. We continued up another hour until it seemed we had reached a dead-end. The incline had gone from difficult but gradual to nearly straight up.

'Well, fuck, Marines. This doesn't look good,' said the Squad Leader.

'I know I don't have to say it, but how the hell are we getting up that without ropes and shit. That's a fucking wall, bro,' said Corporal Diego.

Corporal Murphy said nothing and just looked in disgust at Corporal Williams, whose head hung low and made no eye contact with anyone.

'Gents, let's take five, get some water down, and I'll have a think on this shit show,' said the Squad Leader.

As the group rested, I inspected the wall. From their perspective, I could see why they thought it was not climbable, but I had gone up worse without ropes. Really, the main problem I saw was the extra weight from all the armour, weapons, extra ammo, and heavy backpacks full of more extra ammo, mortar rounds, water, and food. I decided not to ask – I just began to climb.

'What the fuck?! How the hell did he get up there?' said the Squad Leader looking up at me.

'What the fuck, Boot!?' said Corporal Murphy.

'Shit, he's getting up that quick,' said Corporal Diego.

Before they noticed me, I had made it a quarter of the way up the cliff, and a few minutes later, I reached the top of the ledge. It was a fairly flat space about the size of a Humvee, with a sharp drop of at least 500 feet on the other side. There was another wall on the corner, which looked climbable.

I climbed back down and reported it to them. I told them that I had experience in climbing, and that if they let me take their armour and packs one by one, I could get it all up the top and they would be able to scale the wall much easier. With no other option, the Squad Leader said yes. Corporal Murphy did not seem thrilled with the idea, but he said nothing more than a grunt and a spit. One by one, I took their gear off them, and had them follow me up the 50-foot wall to the top of the ledge. Huntly tried to take his own gear up, but then he struggled and nearly fell, and I had to get it off him.

I had carried all but Corporal Williams' load to the top, came back down, and was very tired from it. I should have taken a rest, but I let my pride get me and I took his load as well. The pack was the heaviest of them yet, was filled with live mortar rounds, and it hurt my back as I put it on. It made me feel a little bad for how they had treated Corporal Williams – it was so heavy and soaking wet with his sweat. But then he did not even bother saying thank you or noticing me and began scrambling up the wall on his own.

I followed up slowly and was becoming more and more weary, when Corporal Williams – who was climbing very carelessly – kicked at a bit of rock which became dislodged and flew down hitting me in the face with fragments getting into my eyes. I leaned against the wall and tried to whip my eyes with my right hand and holding on with the left. The camo paint was also getting in with all the sweat. I had cleared it well enough to see again when my left arm suddenly started to lose muscle control and against my will my fingers released their grip on the hold in the rock. I reached with my right as I began to fall backwards fully extending it but not getting hold of anything. I knew I was going to fall now and probably die. If the bombs in the pack did not explode on impact and I managed to catch myself, maybe I would not roll down as far as Corporal Williams' helmet. Maybe then I would just be a cripple.

For some reason, I had an interior thought rush to me in that second to say a prayer to St. Michael the Archangel – the patron saint of the Marine Corps – when I thought his name, like I was being pushed from behind, I went forward with a thump against the wall and caught hold of it. For the next half minute, I stayed there holding on shocked by what had just happened. I had had some demonic experiences in the past – crosses flying off the wall and that sort of thing – but never anything good or helpful.

'Hey, you alright down there, Brodie?' called Corporal Diego.

'Yeah, I am fine, Corporal.'

'Good, now stop fuckin' around and get your ass up here ya fuckin' spider monkey,' called down Corporal Murphy.

I climbed up and met them on the top. I tried asking if they had seen what just happened, but they had been opening MREs and had started eating. Huntly and Chad offered me the Skittles out of their MREs as a thank you, but I said no thanks. I was still quite disturbed by what had just happened, but then the Squad Leader gathered us around and spoke on the further plan. And like how so often an important or unique thing is fully in view and seemly will never leave, the thought of it was stored away, and attention came to the present task.

It was decided that we would form whatever sort of defensive position on the ledge as we could for the time being. We were still totally open to the main bit of Safarak but at least we had some cover from the next wall face. Corporal Murphy and Corporal Diego were to leave their packs with us and climb the next wall and assess the possibility of any further ascent. There were maybe two hours left of light and the shadow of the mountain made it much darker. They went up and over the wall whilst we set all the packs in a crescent formation to provide a little more cover.

An hour later, Corporal Murphy radioed down to us that it was hopeless. At the top of that wall, they saw a ravine with a 300-foot drop and then another wall going up to at least 500-feet. Even with climbing gear, it would be impossible to do in what day light we had left. And even if it was possible, it seemed there may be more similar walls, drops, and peaks before ever reaching the main citadel of the mountain. The Squad Leader decided that we should consider the mission a failure and bed down for the night. He radioed Command telling them that we made it as far as we could, and we were taking defensive positions for the night.

Corporal Murphy and Corporal Diego would not be able to safely make it down to us in the failing light and took up a position where they could. Command ordered them to fire a 203 flare to note their position – despite the fact that it would surely also alert the Taliban to where they were. As the dark embraced the dessert, a red star cluster shot up into the night.

'There's your fireworks, gents! Happy 4th of July, Marines!' said the Squad Leader.

Chad and Huntly spoke about patriotism and how that flare which slowly descended to the base of the mountain reminded them of why we were there and what we were fighting for. The talk reminded me of a memory at the School of Infantry when a band played the Star-Spangled Banner at some ceremony. After they had finished, one of the Marines next to me turned to another and spoke of how he still got goosebumps and felt his heart warm whenever he heard that play – just as he had as a child. I had never felt anything when hearing it played. Nothing at all. Not even some echo of pride. I wanted to and I wanted to be a part of the whole American thing, but I did not and was not. Maybe it came from growing up Alaskan, but none of it meant anything to me. I was there as a matter of honour. The country I lived in was in a time of War and I knew I was able to do it, so I did. I was not going to let another guy die in my place and there was honour in this. And though I was sure that there were likely many Americans who saw me now as some sort of patriotic American hero – I was not. It was not about America for me – even if I wanted it to be – I was just too honest with myself about it to claim otherwise and so whenever such conversations came up, I remained silent. Good for them at least, I guess. This thought was interrupted by the Squad Leader:

'Gents, we are going to set up a Firewatch. Each of us will sit an hour and when the sun comes up, Murp and Diego will come back down to us, and then we'll get the fuck off this rock. I'll take first watch. Get some rest and make sure your night vison is working.'

The shadow of the mountain and the constant wind had cooled us down quite a bit and it was almost comfortable to lie on the rock. As soon as I put my head down on a water bottle for a pillow, I was asleep. I awoke some hours later to Corporal Williams poking me with his foot.

'Hey Boot, you're on watch next. When your hour is up, it's Huntly's turn.'

'Yes, Corporal.'

I checked my rifle – round in the chamber, weapon of safe – then put on my NVGs. The mountain was dark with little light from the waxing crescent moon, but the stars were all very bright. I switched on the NVGs and the mountain became green. I began to scan for Taliban. The mountain felt hostile and not at all desolate, like some spirit of ancient wrath dwelt there and watched me. I thought I saw something move every now and then, but it would turn out to be nothing. I would see a shape like a man hiding in a cave, but then it would be just a shadow. Then I heard a horrible sound like evil laughter coming up from the desert floor below. Corporal Diego also heard it and would later describe it as sounding like a retard laughing. I took out my bayonet and attached it to my rifle.

'Brodie, did you just fix bayonets?' said Corporal Williams who was apparently not asleep yet.

'Yes, Corporal.'

'And why ya do that? You see Taliban or something sketchy?'

'There is some sort of strange animal laughing in the rocks below.'

'Laughing? Shit, that's just a Desert fox, Boot.'

The next day, Corporal Murphy and Corporal Diego rejoined us, and we descended to the base of the mountain. Near the bottom, we found Corporal Williams' helmet, and then walked along the base until we met up with the other group of climbers. It turned out that they had a similar result as us and did not make it much higher up before bedding down. The mission was a failure on the part of our Command and really the only intel we gathered was that the mountain was probably too difficult for the Taliban to climb – otherwise we would have all been killed in the night.

As we rode in the Armadillo back to the FOB, a very fatigued Corporal Murphy offered me a cigarette, saying nothing. I had smoked a tobacco pipe and sometimes a cigar for over a year at that point, but I had never inhaled before. Corporal Murphy said whilst lighting it for me:

'Good job up there, Boot.'

And then I inhaled the smoke.

Printed in Great Britain
by Amazon